KAAKNU THE VOLVON

a novel

James Benney

Rocky Ridge Publications

All Rights Reserved.

No part of this publication
may be reproduced
or transmitted in any form whatsoever,
without permission in writing
from the author.

Visit: www.jamesbenney.com

ISBN-13: 978-0-9838480-2-8
ISBN-10: 0983848025

Copyright © 2012 James Benney
Published 2012
Second Edition 2013

Design & Layout: Crawshaw Design
Cover and Map Art: John Finger
Editorial Consultant: Robyn Russell

Rocky Ridge Publications

Printed in the United States of America

Introduction

Kaaknu the Volvon tribal chieftan was a real person. Recorded history shows that he attained prominent stature during his lifetime, which started in 1770 in a benign 10,000 year-old Native American cultural environment around Mount Diablo, east of the San Francisco Bay.

In thirty-five short years he saw the complete dissolution of his tribe and the total loss of all of their ancestral territory to Spanish soldiers and settlers and the Jesuit Missions. He died in 1826 at Mission San Jose. Very little is known about him.

Here I have imagined a life story, built around known historical events and my own familiarity with the land Kaaknu was raised on and lived for the first 35 years of his life.

The Volvon tribal territory remains virtually untouched today. Many village and camp sites lie undisturbed in the Black Hills behind Mount Diablo, part of the Morgan Territory Regional Preserve. One can still walk the paths he walked, and see the same panoramic views of central California that he saw.

My hope is that more people will begin to appreciate the fantastic cultural stability that his people managed to sustain through hundreds of generations.

In November of 1969, hundreds of Native Americans swarmed over Alcatraz Island and occupied it for the next eighteen months. This action marked the visible beginning of a resurgence of interest in what had mistakenly been thought of as a lost culture.

James Benney
2012

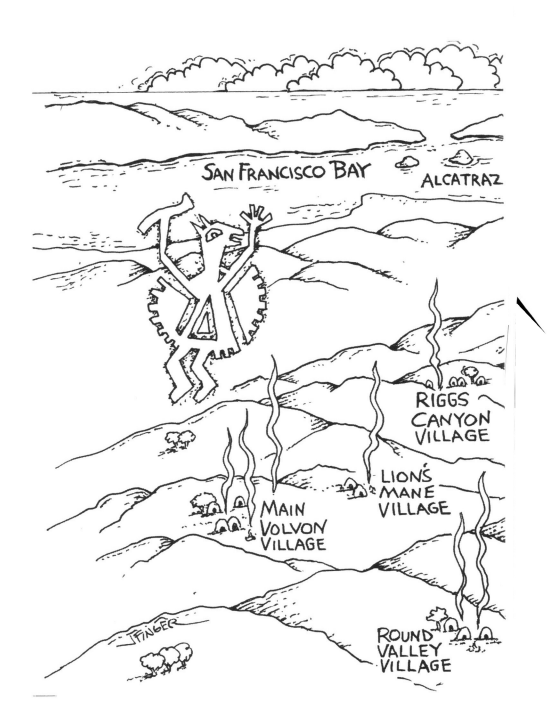

KAAKNU THE VOLVON

Prologue

Circling the birthing site in upper Deer Valley, just south of Antioch, California, the peregrine falcon peers down. Dawn is breaking in the distance, the screaming has subsided, and a hushed silence has fallen over the morning. Coyotes stand watch on the hillside. The year is 1770. Kaaknu, the chief's son, is born, minutes before sunrise envelopes the hills.

The Volvon shaman Jalquin suddenly appears in the first light, his body painted in extraordinary patterns with clay, cinnabar, and charcoal from burned poison oak. His hair gleams dark as obsidian, his gaunt frame and sunken cheekbones a startling reflection of the ascetic lifestyle he has chosen to lead. His arms resemble wilted branches.

As long as the villagers could remember, no man had ever been allowed at the birthing site, and a tremor of fear and anticipation rippled through the air. The old women and the midwives pause, the rags they've used in the birth gathered in their chapped hands. Jalquin, who lives on the mountain, Diablo, has not been seen for several years—not by his own tribe, nor by anyone else's. He is as much a myth as a man.

The women step back, acknowledging his approach. Kaaknu is at his mother Muwekma's breast, his thin thatch of dark hair oily with afterbirth. Jalquin settles his eyes on the child and squints in the early light. When at last he looks up, he locks eyes with each of the surrounding women before circling the newborn and chanting, his hands like birds dancing around his feathered head. His voice rises with the sun, his story of the First People unraveling in rhythmic song. The women listen intently. The newborn closes his eyes.

*　*　*

Back in the Volvon village, high on the Black Hills plateau, Kaaknu's father, the Volvon chief Miwok, stares skyward in awe, gratitude, and apprehension. His child is healthy. His wife is alive. And yet.

A slender, tawny black-tailed deer darts behind a curtain of brush. The animals, Miwok knows, can only sense what is happening; the people recognize it in their bones. Unparalleled change is upon Miwok's people. Strangers from the seas and from the south are starting to appear in nearby tribal territories. Tales of brutality have swept north to the Black Hills. Miwok often wakes to the terrified gasps of troubled dreams.

He lifts his head. The peregrine falcon hovers near the golden hills before taking flight, gliding back into time, before people, its wings folding and unfolding as it ascends towards the heavens.

* * *

Jalquin sings. It is 15,000 years earlier. North America is not inhabited by people but is overflowing with primeval wildlife. The falcon soars north, and peers back across the Bering Straits into Siberia and Outer Mongolia.

The earth shifts beneath its wings, entering a warming phase that will dramatically alter the landscape. The Mongols have evolved over the ages in a harsh, frigid environment. Cold is no stranger to them. As the land warms, new habitable freshwater sites appear like mirages in what was once frozen tundra. Sprouts of green edible food spring from the earth where impenetrable glaciers once stood. Some of the Mongols move east to take advantage of these new resources.

The falcon travels forward a hundred generations. The planet has continued to warm, and small groups of people have moved slowly across the now fertile Bering Straits into what is now the vast landscape of Alaska. Hundreds of more generations will pass before people discover the inviting and undisturbed ecosystem that was North America at this time.

Rivers in North America teem with countless varieties of freshwater and saltwater fish. Herds of antelope, elk, and deer wander freely. Whole hillsides bloom with edible grapes and berries; nutritious bulbs flourish unattended. The abundance is remarkable. Word spreads back through the chain of islands and village sites, and adventurers from every nomadic tribe in the far north of Mongolia set forth for the New World.

People settle on every piece of habitable land near fresh water, their numbers exploding, their expansion seemingly unstoppable. They bring with them valuable knowledge they've acquired as they've traversed the Northern lands, finding now, in every micro-environment, new plants, new animals, new varieties of shellfish and fresh water organisms.

The falcon soars on. It is a thousand years after people first crossed the Bering Straits. A group of explorers finds their way into California's lush Central Valley and follows the immense Sacramento River downstream to where it meets the San Joaquin River. The wealth of food and water is unbelievable. A land rush of Native Americans ensues not unlike the Gold Rush that will later occur in 1849.

Scores of full tribal families make their homes in the area. Scouts scour the hills and streams while Mount Diablo looms four thousand feet above it all. Early ancestors of the Volvon tribe move up into the hills and come across the plateau now known as the Black Hills, directly east of the enormous mountain. Year-round spring water, ample game, grasslands and oak woodlands—along with ideal defensive positions and escape routes—makes for comfortable living and a reliable lifestyle. The people settle in for generations.

10,000 years before Kaaknu's birth a drought on the West Coast brings complications that last three full generations for the Native Americans. A cloud of dust and debris swaths the parched earth. Plants wither, animals pass away, many people perish. Miraculously, certain areas are partially spared due to their unique geographic location and the continuing availability of some essential resources, especially fresh water.

The land around the confluence of the Sacramento and San Joaquin Rivers is one such area, the Delta surrounding it surpassing the Tigris and Euphrates in richness and diversity. Several Volvon ancestors living in the Black Hills survive the catastrophic drought and over time become known as the First People, with Mount Diablo as the center point of their creation.

The peregrine falcon navigates the next hundred centuries. Below him, Indians thrive. Spectacular vistas from the mountain shimmer in their view. Food grows in abundance around them. Pine nuts and manzanita berries prosper. Traders from distant tribes come to share in these resources, and legendary tales of the First People spread throughout Central California. People come to Mount Diablo for the Volvon's extraordinary ceremonies and trading opportunities, as well as important weddings, baptisms and vision quests.

This world remains connected and intact for the next 10,000 years. The California Indians survive drought, earthquakes, wildfires, and all manner of other natural and man-made disasters.

The falcon returns to the present. Jalquin the shaman suddenly turns away from the birthing site, his voice caught in the still morning air. It is not a natural catastrophe that is soon to be upon them. He disappears at once to return to his redoubt in the oak copses near the summit of Mount Diablo.

The falcon soars above him. No one speaks. The child sleeps; the birds cry out in wonder.

Part 1

I

Chief Miwok knows Kaaknu's birth is a blessing but also an uncertain omen. That morning, he meets with the elders from several adjoining tribes in the sweat lodge at the main Volvon village, which overlooks the Brushy Peak trading grounds. The domed hut is warm from the heat emanating from the rocks on the fire. Chupcans, Saclans, Ssaoms, and Carquins undress and bask in the heat.

Part of their universal shared mythologies include stories of fearsome tribes far to the south who were subdued by foreign conquerors who had arrived in huge ships. The names Vizcaino and Cortez are alien to them but the results of their invasions have rippled outward like the waves from a stone dropped in a pond.

Miwok has called the meeting to discuss his son's role in their future and to psychologically prepare the other leaders for sudden change. First, though, the tribal leaders find themselves recalling the past. While they scrape their bodies with bone tools, the elders recount the appearance of Sir Francis Drake in Marin County two hundred years earlier. Miwok listens, although he knows the tale well—in 1568, Sir Francis Drake in his Spanish galleon came ashore in western Marin. He and his sailors were there for three weeks, during which word of their arrival spread for hundreds of miles inland.

Drake and his sailors were equipped in a manner that was beyond the Indians' comprehension. Miwok pauses, calling to mind the metal swords, fine fabrics and gold coins that were marveled at during that time. He imagines the ship that was thought of as phenomenal, its grand white sails billowing in the gales north of the Golden Gate.

When they departed, the trade goods they left behind, including glass beads and belt buckles, became mysterious, valuable totems to those who possessed them. But also left behind were unfamiliar diseases that spread rapidly through the population, diseases the medicine doctors and shamans, who relied on sucking, herbs, and ancient rituals, were unable to cure. A disease that became known as measles decimated hundreds of people in adjoining villages, all of them dying agonizing deaths. Venereal disease swelled like a fast-moving tide. Sir Francis Drake's appearance portended what would occur in Miwok's lifetime.

Over the next two centuries, the elders went on, there were many reports of sightings of large vessels going up and down the California coast. Subsequent landings of other explorers intensified the concerns of the people. Yet nothing had compared to the arrival in 1769, just the year prior, of the Jesuit missionaries and Spanish soldiers in Monterey, who came to stay with their cattle, sheep, and horses, and muskets, swords, and guns.

Chief Miwok and the elders recall watching this caravan arrive from the hills above Monterey. They were hidden from view but possessed the advantage of closely observing every movement, every activity. It was a three-day walk back to the Volvon village but Miwok wouldn't leave until he had grasped the situation as best as he could. These intruders were eventually coming towards Volvon territory, and he could do little to halt them.

From the sweat lodge, he watches as his radiant wife carries Kaaknu into the village. Her thick braids dangle near her waist. He has loved her for many years, since first glimpsing her chiseled face at the Brushy Peak trading ground. She appeared to have been carved by the hands of gods. Now she held in her hands their newborn son, whose eyes, when they briefly flutter open, are the color of walnuts. The elders pause mid-sentence; the villagers stop mid-task. Love rushes through him before terror snakes up his spine. Even though all the lookout posts had more helpers during this important birthing time, up and down the ridgelines, one had to ask: Who still dared to bring a child into this world?

Decisions among the elders continued to be made while the creek near the sweat lodge rushed past, swelled by the recent rains. The warning signs, one of the nine chiefs who are gathered in the sweat lodge says, have been present for seven generations. But now the intrusive press of events, out of their control, is being felt strongly among all the people. Still, another chief argues, everything appears normal. The seasons, he says, arms arced upward towards the sky, come and go. The Creator provides food and water; shelter is easily constructed. All this is true, Miwok thinks. The day-to-day workings of his tribe continue on, as they have through countless centuries of births and deaths.

The elders are well aware of the Mission being constructed in Monterey, and the previous Missions built as far south as San Diego. They have heard about the soldiers astride horses, their bright shiny goods, their new religion with priests and prayers and rosaries and Indian slave labor, bells pealing at daybreak in a call for Mass. Some of Miwok's more aggressive tribal neighbors were formulating strategies to stop the spread of these unwelcome strangers and the sicknesses they brought with them. Meanwhile, many Indians from the south had moved north and east to avoid contact with this new world. Miwok believed there were now about a thousand Volvons living in the Black Hills, and they had already absorbed some of these refugees.

Kaaknu, however, would be raised in the old ways, certainly one of the last to do so. He was the chief's son, after all, and it comforted Miwok to know that even amid great anxiety and change, his child would be given special care to ensure that he ate well and slept well and was protected as much as possible from the worries of the world around him. The old medicine woman Julpina would come up from the hollow and perform rituals for Kaaknu's benefit, burning leaves of yarrow, wild cucumber, wormwood and jimson weed along with rare and sacred herbs and spices while waving the smoking medicine basket over his treasured head and body. Miwok listened as the elders talked quietly.

Jalquin and his entourage arrive from the shaman's lair the following day. Jalquin, ornamented in a headdress of bird feathers—heron, mallard, song sparrow—chants a short prayer and then returns immediately to his redoubt near the top of the mountain. His chant is a rare gift but his unusual appearance in the village is a dire warning.

During the night, a mild earthquake rumbles through the village. A pair of boulders spring loose from the cliff above and bound down and over the village's protective rock and bay tree barrier, erected precisely to stop falling rocks like these from entering the central living grounds.

Both boulders clear the barrier and land in the middle of the main promenade. The sleeping villagers stumble out of their wiki-up dwellings, morning dew glistening on the surrounding oak trees. To Miwok's tremendous relief, no one is hurt. But as the day unfolds, as the robins and mourning doves sing with the rising sun, the villagers begin to view the rocks as a message somehow related to Kaaknu's arrival in the world. It is unclear what the incident portends but its significance is not denied. The boulders are left in place.

These stones will be the last two rocks Kaaknu touches the final time he is allowed by the Mission padres to visit his village fifty-four years later. By then, to the Volvon villagers they will have come to represent the inevitable disruption of their people.

Muwekma holds Kaaknu tightly to her chest, and kneels closer to the fire.

II

Kaaknu's earliest memories are of the fire in the center of his family's wiki-up, ruby and gold and blue-tinged flames a seeming constant. He remembers soft warm blankets, worn rabbit skins used as pillows, and the rich aromas of home, acorn soup, and fresh walnut bread. He recalls the villagers moving about, each with their own special responsibilities for the whole tribe, as well as for themselves. Images will often return to him when he is older, of flint knappers making arrowheads, bulb gatherers returning with brodiaea and soaproot, the piles of firewood at the village's edge, the women with children in their arms, others harvesting berries and seeds. He will remember hillsides being burned to the ground on purpose, which his father told him stimulated and controlled favored plant species.

As he matured, Kaaknu came to understand that any sign of life—fire, the scent of food cooking, the sound of lovemaking, the gurgle of the creek—meant life for the people. This, above all, was what mattered. Kaaknu was taught that the Volvon tribe's gift was special because of their association with the great sacred mountain, Diablo, and the ancient rituals and ceremonies of the First People that had survived and evolved generation after generation.

His father Miwok waits. The peregrine waits. It seems to Kaaknu that the whole village is waiting. Kaaknu understands that he is an important son, borne from a vital man, thrust into an uncertain time. Around the campfire, Kaaknu as a child hears snatches of stories about famines, birth defects, droughts, earthquakes, fires and disease. Also, occasional brutal massacres have occurred, and now there is subjugation of Indians by arrogant white men. The imported cattle that have arrived with these foreigners are grazing away at the people's lifeblood food resources on the hillsides. Always be ready for anything, he hears his people say. That is the way.

Miwok's shoulders seem always tense, his back bent, as if the entire weight of the tribe's future rests on his shoulders. Kaaknu lies down on the stack of blankets his mother has set up for him. In the mornings, he will wake up with his mother Muwekma at his side, weaving baskets before standing to prepare his first meal of the day. Later, they will leave the village to gather grains and seeds and bulbs and berries that have become harvestable in the surrounding hills. They will return to the village before nightfall, watching the home fires burn in their rightful places.

In the summer months following Kaaknu's birth, news had spread further throughout the Central California tribes of the Catholic Mission and town being set up in Monterey. The penetration of the Portola Expedition in 1772 up the San Francisco Peninsula and into the East Bay hills near where the Volvons lived had heightened concerns.

Many chiefs had greeted the Portola excursion. They traded items with the strangers, from animal skins and spears to charmstones that were rumored to possess auspicious powers, for buttons, buckles, and rope. Some chiefs quickly became familiar with the brutally offensive stance taken by the Spanish troops. It was critical, they said, to be cautious around the dangerous guns and swords wielded by these new people.

The Volvon people had traded with the tribes from Monterey Bay since the beginning of time. But now, daily reports on the Spanish and Jesuit doings were reaching Chief Miwok. It was the consistency of these reports that alarmed him and his people. He had known about the colonialists for some time, but this was an egregious entry into the region. Miwok often traveled there to observe them from the hills above and to gather knowledge.

In August of that year, he left Kaaknu and his wife for Monterey. He stayed out of sight above the bustling New World community, being built with what appeared to be mostly Indian labor. On those nights in the hills above the ocean, he couldn't sleep. The waning moon cast shadows in the trees. Every creak of a branch sent his heart into a spasm, as if his chest were full of bees. The Spaniards had horses and could travel near to his tribe's territory in a single day. This was of utmost concern to him.

In November of the same year, Lieutenant Pedro Fages's expedition came all the way up the Fremont Plain, just to the west of Volvon territory. Sparse and sporadic resistance from Indians was not going to deter El Oso (The Bear) and his people. Miwok was summoned that autumn to observe the movement of this expedition.

It was unstoppable. The year Kaaknu turned two, the Fages-Crespi expedition left the Presidio in Monterey. They headed along the south and east shores of San Francisco Bay all the way to the Carquinez Straights and Crockett, home of the Carquin Indians.

Miwok learned of this and hurried with several members of his tribe to the primary village of the Carquins. This was the crossing point to get to Solano and Napa Counties from Contra Costa County, and the Carquins controlled both sides of the Sacramento River Estuary as well as the adjoining hills. Their skill at maneuvering Tule boats across the channel to Glen Cove in Vallejo was unparalleled. Their knowledge of the currents and conditions on the water had been fine-tuned over many centuries.

Miwok remained in the hills with many other braves while hundreds of Indians—up to four hundred, Miwok guessed—greeted Fages and Crespi and their small contingent as they rode into the village, their European facial skin pale in the light. Chupcans, Tatcans, and Yokuts had come to observe and participate in this interaction with the foreigners, and to ensure that they didn't penetrate any further into

Central California without meeting fierce resistance.

Miwok and his men were not seen as the day unfolded. Below them they watched their fellow natives surround the expedition but their actions were soon blurred by a net of fog. The fog thinned at nightfall and then Miwok was able to watch the group dine on a feast prepared by the Carquins. Huge burritos, which Miwok knew would be stuffed with meats, seeds, nuts, and fruit, were shared by nine Indian chiefs in complete regalia and the small party of Spanish explorers.

This peace will not last, Miwok said to his men. The next morning, they followed the Fages expedition step by step as it made its way back down through the Diablo and San Ramon valleys. The Volvons' return to their territory was lonesome and quiet. They did not discuss the disturbing thoughts whirling in their heads. Miwok briefly thought of the winter ahead—the rains and winds, the smattering of snow that might fall on Jalquin's redoubt near the top of Mount Diablo. As he walked, the usual preparations needed for the winter crossed his mind and then escaped him. His tribe's long-term future—so uncertain, so fraught with worry—was consuming him.

Seven days after they had left, they got back to the main village. Miwok reached for his wife. He wanted to talk but found that words escaped him. She was silent and contemplative during their evening meal but as darkness descended on the village, and they sat quietly while Kaaknu slept, she told him of the tribal runners who had come to their village while he was away. They had told her it wouldn't be long before she, too, would have to confront the conquerors.

III

The year is 1773. Kaaknu wakes to the birth of Mala's daughter. His village is alive with activity. It has rained for weeks. Now, without the constant downpours, the people seem to be reborn in the morning sunlight. Fires burn in the center of the promenade. Acorn granaries dot the landscape. Several men huddle near the edge of the compound, sharpening their tools. Women rustle by, infants in baskets cradled at their chests.

His mother combs his hair with her fingers and a soaproot brush. Today, his father will take him to the Brushy Peak trading grounds for the first time. Miwok walks beside the three year-old Kaaknu towards Livermore's Altamont Pass. Quail and cotton tail rabbits scurry in the thicket. A coyote's wild bark rings out.

The variety of goods available at the trade site astonishes young Kaaknu. Spearheads, fish traps, and a vast selection of food, herbs and medicines. He is mesmerized by the goods that change hands all day long as traders come and go. Olivella shells seem to have particular value and are used like money.

His father takes his hand and shows him some items their tribe has never seen before. Ceramic buttons, exquisite beads, mantles and metal coins. Miwok points out the dried and seasoned beef and lamb dangling from the hands of several traders. These, Miwok says, are from the Spanish and Mexicans in Monterey. Kaaknu is given a taste of the jerky. It is foreign in his mouth, but unforgettable. Meanwhile, his father is engaged in a conversation with an Ohlone chief. Intruders, Kaaknu hears them say. Change. Massacre.

Kaaknu is confused and exhilarated on their walk home. All the different impressions! The things he saw and tasted! His father nods, contemplative and sullen. A mile away from their village Miwok pauses. He kneels down in the dirt and holds his child's chin in his warm, thick hands.

"Kaaknu," he says. "Fully armed explorers have penetrated our territory around Mount Diablo twice since your birth. There is every indication that some of them will arrive in our village any time now."

Kaaknu nods, while his young mind churned, thinking perhaps it would be possible for these new people to learn to live with them and share in the bounty of the Creator.

As if sensing his son's thoughts, Miwok says, "They don't respect the ways of our people. They have their own ideas, their own resources. And the Indians who have come into contact with them are now dying in great numbers." Miwok sweeps his hand from the north to the south. "Diseases we've never before experienced are rushing through the villages. They call us heathen savages. They call us filthy animals, and they want to convert us to their religion and remove us from our homes, even though we are not a warring people. Do you understand, son?"

Miwok gathers his satchel of goods from the ground and they continue their walk. Kaaknu's feet are blackened with blisters. In the distance, Muwekma raises her hand in greeting. They are almost home.

Miwok's words prove to be true. In the spring of 1776, Kaaknu is taken to the Diablo Valley to observe the passing of the De Anza expedition. It had already been to San Francisco to find a site for the new Mission there; now, it was headed up around Mount Diablo following the footsteps of the Fages-Crespi route. The mountain itself and the Black Hills plateau in Morgan Territory had thus far remained safe. Missionized Indian scouts leading the Spanish reported mysterious malevolent forces in the vicinity of Mount Diablo and were afraid to show the soldiers a way up. From the hills above Concord, Kaaknu watched as the De Anza troop rode by in the valley. Hundreds of

Indians were in the hills to watch as well. Only a handful had remained in the lower camps and villages to greet and interact with the newcomers.

It had become abundantly clear in recent years to avoid these soldiers whenever possible. They would shoot the native people with their metal guns, or maim them with their swords. Blood drenched the ground. Screams were heard for miles. The smoke of cremated bodies from Indian ceremonies for the dead tainted the air.

Recently, the Yelamu tribe in San Francisco had been driven out of all of their historical villages completely, and had either fled in Tule boats to the North Bay or the East Bay, or were working as indentured servants in the Mission, their daughters' virginity marked by tattoos on their thighs. No longer did fresh fish from the San Francisco Bay and coastline make its way to the Brushy Peak trading grounds. No longer did natives from the North Bay and East Bay dare to venture onto the San Francisco Peninsula.

Kaaknu watches. The De Anza expedition doesn't stop at the Carquin village in Crockett as the last expedition did. They continue, riding around the whole mountain of Diablo, stirring fear throughout the region. When Kaaknu returns home, there is terror in his mother's dark eyes. The villagers are quiet and tense; they do not smile. They know that this is truly the beginning of the end.

From the warmth of his wiki-up, Kaaknu observes some of the Volvon families packing up their essential belongings. Several are going north up the Central Valley, where the white man has not yet penetrated. Those who have chosen to stay behind bid them farewell. Some have decided to stay in the East Bay hills and hold on, even if it means battling to their deaths.

Soon, fewer members of other tribes will still come to Volvon territory for the traditional dances and ceremonies. The harvest will lose strength, because fewer people are around to do the harvesting. Management of resources will falter. In the following year, a band of Mexican settlers will start the town of San Jose. Ancient fires will stop burning. Traders from the affected areas will no longer come to Brushy Peak. Indian escapees from the Missions will be searched for by armed soldiers and brought back, or killed. Local native collaborators in the Missions will curry favor by reporting on the likely whereabouts of those who have escaped. The foreigners will move in closer and closer to Mount Diablo and the Black Hills.

IV

The summer of Kaaknu's tenth year, after being immersed throughout his childhood in the legends, lore, and practical survival skills of the Volvon, he is granted permission to accompany Yokun, one of the long-distance traders, and several others on a trek into the Sierra Nevada. They would be gone for three months.

Kaaknu glanced around his village as he prepared for the journey. The number of people in his village had diminished significantly in the past few years. Back in the summer of 1776, a large party of Spanish priests, soldiers, and settlers left Monterey for San Francisco, where they built a Mission and a Presidio. Resistance by Native Americans was quelled by shooting and killing or arresting and whipping. The first baptisms of Indians occurred.

The year after, 1777, Kaaknu and Miwok had traveled to the hills above San Jose to observe the development of the new Mexican settlers' homesteads. They kept a safe distance out of fear of being captured. Spanish supply ships rose like ghosts on the horizon, and were now arriving in San Francisco Bay on an annual basis. Kaaknu fell asleep that night to the sound of horses in his ears, knowing, even at that young age, that the Spaniards could make it into his territory in far less time than he and his father could by walking. He had been eager to get home.

Returning to the Volvon village the next day, Miwok and the elders made final decisions on who would go north, and who would stay behind. Kaaknu and his mother and father would stay. Most of the older people would go, while some of the younger families would stay to see the change through to its end. No one, it was decided, would go to the Missions.

When the Missionaries came to Santa Clara and began recruiting natives to build the Mission there, Kaaknu's father sent more

Volvon families away to hopefully safer terrain. Long-standing truces and intermarriages between tribes determined the best places for certain people to go to protect themselves from what was coming.

Kaaknu felt the emptiness of his village profoundly as he got ready for his trip east with the trader. He peered up at the great mountain. His tribe possessed a spiritual connection to and metaphysical understanding of the world that other tribes aspired to, and whose source was understood to be the mountain itself. He looked at Mount Diablo, and, closing his eyes, chanted a short prayer for hope, perseverance, clarity, and mercy.

The trek with Yokun is harsh but fascinating. Every tribe, Kaaknu learns, has a niche, an exquisite specialty. He and the traders cross the vast Central Valley from the Altamont Pass in Livermore, winding through swampland, past enormous rivers. Tule boats on the water appear agile and so numerous that there is always someone to assist them through the rough wetter passages. This trail across the great valley, Yokun says, has been used for thousands of years, shifting course with nature's demands but always heading for the same place.

On Kaaknu's side of the path through the valley stands the Brushy Peak trading ground, situated at the border of three major tribal groups; on the other side are tribes that have existed at the confluences of creeks and rivers flowing out of the Sierra Nevada for thousands of years, and have access to unique resources not found at lower elevations. Yokun and the others trade for each tribe's specialized goods while Kaaknu is introduced to customs, practices, and ceremonial gatherings that are foreign to him but no less beautiful and inspiring than those of his own people.

The spoken languages seem to change daily with every new tribe they happen upon. There is a different way of speaking every thirty or forty miles. Still, there is a primeval manner of communicating that seems to work everywhere they go. Signs are exchanged; body language speaks volumes. Greetings that are friendly are easy to decipher, he quickly learns. Greetings that are not are equally transparent. A turn of the head could mean, leave. The smallest of smiles could mean, welcome; please, come into our village.

On his journey, Kaaknu witnesses dances and foods and clothing and feathers and weapons he has never seen before. There are Indians everywhere they go on their three-month trek, too many natives to count. Hunters and gatherers are encountered at every turn. Every clear water stream has settlements up and down the banks. Some villages have a thousand or more people, with another thousand scattered throughout the further reaches of their territory. Occasional chiefs and shamans are frightening to behold, while others appear gentle and kind. Yokun knows most of the people along the way.

Some tribes choose to live in harsh environments, having learned to survive without relying on regular traders. Other tribes are colorful and bawdy—their villages like one on-going celebration of life and love. On this journey, Kaaknu realizes more than ever before that the Volvon tribe has a special place in all of this, and that is to observe and communicate the larger metaphysical picture of Indian society and history to all the native peoples. That is why all these other tribal people came to Volvon territory every year in waves. Winter, spring, summer and fall, his village was filled with people keen on being a part of the traditional ceremonies. Mount Diablo and the First People were revered by all.

While traveling with Yokun, Kaaknu also realizes that most people are afraid to go up to the top of the mountain itself. One didn't just hike up. One was led through a series of experiences at the lower levels and then only with prior approval would he or she be escorted to the top to meet with the shamans. Interlopers were not tolerated and often disappeared, or returned as mad men, no longer able to cope with normal Indian society, hidden by their families for the rest of their lives. One had to prepare properly for this spiritual experience.

Kaaknu's adventure across the vast valley and into the Sierra Nevada mountains was part of that preparation. His birthright was part of it and his early trips into the sweat lodge were part of it. Kaaknu will be instructed to stay off the upper mountain until he is invited and led through the crucial ritual processes by Jalquin and Wek Wek the falcon shaman and their acolytes. But nothing will prepare him for what is to come to his people in his lifetime. His entire tribe will go from complete freedom to total subjugation and expulsion from their homeland in a matter of thirty-five years. Fully extirpated.

He came home to his village concerned about the future but bursting with enthralling tales, in his hands an extraordinary gift basket for his mother, which could not be replicated with their local materials. He is often filled with apprehension but he's still a young boy, and his mother and father encourage him to relish his youth. He plays hide and seek with the other children in the rocks near the creek behind the village. He learns to be wary of rattlesnakes and grizzly bears. He finds a baby bird without its mother and nurses it to health in a nest he fashions out of twigs and feathers. Even while disaster looms in the clouds above Mount Diablo, in the Black Hills the salty ocean air from the west and the spectacular scenery make every day glorious. The Volvons still wake before dawn to watch the sun rise in dazzling bands of pinks and yellows over the Central Valley. To arise alive is always a blessing.

Part 2

1

Kaaknu dreams of peering down at the San Francisco Bay before him, a glob of green and mahogany browns that gives way to a rough, charcoal ocean. The sea sweeps in, and ghost ships bob and flicker on the horizon. Through the mist, he sees a cross, an Indian child in spoiled rags, smoke rising from burial grounds. He shifts in his sleep. A young woman, familiar in her gait, stands behind a willow, eyeing him. Her plaited braids fall to her waist and in his dream, Kaaknu sees her tender pink scalp at the severe part in her hair. Arrows suddenly fall to the ground, kicking up dust as they plunge to the earth, their tips spotted with blood darker than night. Jalquin is all at once beside him, holding a baby bird in his bony hands. The bird is close to death, Jalquin says with his eyes. Time is running out, he seems to say. When Kaaknu blinks, the baby bird turns into a falcon.

He wakes with a startle. The morning spills open in front of him, the sun against a violet sky. Branches of oaks are black in silhouette, like curled lace against the grassy hills. He smells burning sage, the spice of jimsom weed, the loamy scent of fresh mud. He wipes his mouth and sits up on the pile of blankets on which he has been resting. Fog creeps among the foothills. Around him, people talk in low syllables, avoiding his eyes. Water boils from a hearth. The old medicine woman Julpina is planted near a fire, her hands cupped against the heat.

She notices that he is awake and bows her head in deference. For weeks now, Kaaknu has been fed especially well, from seasoned elk and stewed roots to thick slabs of fresh walnut bread. The people in the village have stopped talking to him, have stopped acknowledging him. Julpina emerged from the hollow days ago and had her helpers scour the hills and woods for special plants and herbs and seeds, which she will mix in with mud to bathe Kaaknu.

Kaaknu is given a hearty breakfast before the medicine woman and her helpers cleanse him carefully with their strong, sinewy hands.

They peer at his skin, at the groves of trees behind him, above him at the sun, but never at him. He is led to the mud bath Julpina has painstakingly prepared. There, with the scent of earth surrounding him, he lays for an hour. The sky is speckled with clouds. Sage is burned and the smoke waved around him. Julpina's attendants continuously add hot water to the mix to keep the mud from setting. Julpina chants quietly, her wrinkled mouth dropping little gems of prayers and blessings into his ears.

At last he is lifted from the bath and led down to the stream below the village. He rinses off in the ancient swimming hole next to the sweat lodge. The wind tingles sharply against his purified skin. He emerges exhilarated but uncertain of what awaits him. Minutes from now, he will be clothed in traveling gear. He will be escorted from the village by some of the shaman's acolytes. They will not speak to him. The year is 1781. Kaaknu is eleven years old.

His heart quickens on the walk across the wide plateau and down into Round Valley where the fall harvest celebration is taking place. Several tribes from the Delta River area up north have set up camp. As darkness descends, the people embrace the night by dancing in sheer abandonment. He sees flesh, and fire, and stripes of red and black and white paint lining many Indian's limbs like tattoos.

Taken to the prayer circle in the center of the permanent village, he is instructed to sit quietly and fast for three days. The days are endless; the nights exhausting. His mind works furiously as he tries to find peace and calm among the wild chants and music and the sound of feet thumping the ground along with the constant drumming. When he emerges from his fast, he's tired, hungry, and rather delirious. Stars prickle his vision.

He is led to the central campground and fed by the tribal elders.

Although ravenously hungry, a nagging terror keeps him from eating as much as he would like. Immediately, he is taken by the shaman's acolytes five miles back across Volvon Territory to the main approach to the mountain for seekers from the south, the Riggs Canyon Village.

He'll spend another three days here, regaining his strength and participating in spiritual rituals specifically developed to prepare seekers for the journey forward. The atmosphere is a sharp contrast to the surroundings of the prayer circle in Round Valley. Here in the amphitheatre, the mood is serene, the voices subdued. All of this is clearly intended to quiet his mental state. Warm tea made of pine bark and chamomile flowers is almost always at hand. Brief walks through the sunny oak woodlands remind him, wonderfully, of home, but at night his skin becomes goose-bumped and cold, and sore to the touch. His mind is empty during the day, to the point where he feels divinely tranquil, but at night he flails hopelessly with endless thoughts, knowing his father's pressing worries now include his only son's initiation into the shaman's world.

Sleep comes in fits and starts and on the third night, a shaman's acolyte presses his hand softly on Kaaknu's heaving chest. "Hush, child," he whispers, the first words spoken to him since Julpina's mud bath days before. Kaaknu nods but all he can think about is the mountain above him, ascending it foot by foot, mile by mile, and loneliness sweeps through him, vast and deep. It's as if he has opened the door to his family's wiki-up to discover that the whole world has disappeared, that nothing remains, not even air, or light. It's only until he recalls his mother's laughter—the soft ring of it, and her eyes crinkling at the sides—that he is able to steady his mind and drift off into a dreamless sleep.

In the morning, the acolyte reappears. He leads him on to the next phase, further up the mountain. At the Live Oak campground, the air thins and Kaaknu struggles to breathe. Here he will rest for a week and acclimate to the altitude. The others he encounters—the acolyte who quieted him in his sleep, the seekers, the helpers—still don't speak to him. He is fed a diet unusual for him, one mainly of meat and nut proteins, purposely designed to increase his stamina and strength to meet and overcome any strange circumstances he may encounter on his mountain vision quest.

The week passes slowly. He senses from the way the acolyte watches him with a mix of satisfaction and curiosity that he is almost ready for the final ascent. But first he is taken to the Curry Point milling station, where a group of old women witches are presiding over a boiling soup concoction, the likes of which he has never seen or smelled, much less tasted. The women part as he arrives, and he is led to the simmering cauldron. Roots and bulbs bob at the surface of the soup. This, he understands, will be his final meal before ascending the mountain. Kaaknu raises his head. The Devil's Elbow and the summit of Mount Diablo glimmer proudly, dangerously, in the hushed silence. Distended clouds float ominously around the circumference of the mountain top. He finishes his bowl of soup. He knows where he has to go.

The acolyte disappears. The women disappear. Left alone at the milling station with a gourd of water, the last of the fire's flames wrinkle weakly towards the sky. Kaaknu thumbs his wrists, feeling for his pulse. It is faint, and thready. He is unsteady and adrift and terribly lonely.

11

Diablo's mountaintop looms treacherously above. Kaaknu has to climb another two thousand feet through unfamiliar high country. He takes a deep breath and swallows the last mouthful of his tepid water. His toes dig into the earth, finding purchase. He leans momentarily on an oak, though he is feeling stronger; he is feeling that he belongs. He sets off.

The trail winds forward across the near saddle; from there, it appears that the only thing to do is to go up. He has no weapons, no food and, now, no water. He hikes across the open saddle and into a thicket of trees. Amid the pine needles and acorns, the trail he has been following abruptly stops. Four different trails branch off before him, ribboning thinly through the shrub brush.

Kaaknu eyes each one and stretches his neck to see which way they go. It's like looking into a maze with no clear endpoint and impossible to tell which one might lead to the top of the mountain. All of his life, father figures have instructed him to always take the path that best suited him, and to never look back in regret.

Stories of the magic and mystery and terror associated with the upper reaches of Mount Diablo turn in his mind as he stands, riveted, by the choice he has to make. Despite the tales he's heard, no one told him he'd have to make such a fateful decision so soon on the route up. But here it is. Four trails. Kaaknu wonders if they all lead to the top with varying degrees of difficulty. Did only one lead to the top, and the others into detours unimaginable?

He clears his head. He knows it is crucial to open himself up to mysterious forces in this moment. Whatever trail he chooses will foreshadow his path through the rest of his life and the role he'll eventually play in the rapid dissolution of his tribal family's dynamic. He pauses, doubting his preparedness for the perilous journey ahead.

He sits and crosses his legs, and, with his back to the four paths, he looks down the hills in the direction from which he has come. Home is below him—his mother and father, his playmates, his shelter, warmth and food. He imagines his father's face tilted up towards the sky, peering at the mountain with dread and anticipation over his only child's quest.

Here on the mountain the air smells different—colder, crisper, menacing. The sounds are different as well. Hollow and portentous noises, carried in the wind, rush through the trees like noisy apparitions. His eyes rake over the Black Hills below him. He's experienced a wonderful childhood there, marred only by the impending sense of doom that has pervaded his and the nearby villages since before he was born.

He slumps towards the ground. Why is he here? What is the purpose of this fasting and prayer and isolation? Almost immediately he thinks of his father, the great Chief Miwok, who would likely shake his head. You are here, he could hear his father saying, to receive guidance from the spirits as to how to lead your people into the future. He is here because it is his birthright. He was chosen to lead, and trained for it.

Already many of his people had migrated east and north, squeezing themselves into other tribes' territories. No one was going west toward the ocean, nor were they going south. To the east, the snowcapped Sierra Nevada loomed. Life was harsher there, resources not as readily available, but still several of his people with relatives in the mountains were welcomed when they came to the old villages, and given food and shelter.

Mostly, Kaaknu's people were migrating to the north, up the fertile Sacramento River valley. He had to choose a path now and follow it to its end. It was his choice, and his alone. He chose the north trail up the mountain, and did not look back.

Rounding the first corner he sees that the top of the mountain was still miles and miles away. The path he had chosen suddenly ended. Before him lay a quarter mile of tangled manzanita, chemise and buck brush, thicker than any stand of copse he had ever seen. There is no longer a trail but he can't go back. He has to reach the summit, somehow.

Small animal trails left by the raccoons, coyotes, skunks and wood rats who have lived here for millions of years sneak to the right and left, north and south, but there is no visible evidence that a human had ever tried to penetrate this dense thicket. This struck him as strange, and perhaps untrue. A steady stream of seekers who presumably had been led through the same rituals in the lower hills that he had would have probably come to the same four trails he encountered. Yet it appeared that no one had ever gone along this path. He longed to trace his steps back down the mountain but it is an empty, unpromising desire. It is critical to continue on.

He is unable to see the full extent of the thicket from where he stands. It rises above him and clusters tightly down to the ground. His only solution is to crawl into this briar patch on his stomach, his only guidance ascension. Night would arrive soon and he knows progress will be slow, especially if he's going to avoid being torn up by the snags and bramble and broken branches.

Small animals and birds rustle in the undergrowth. After dark, save for help from the moon, he will be vulnerable to these creatures and essentially trapped. He pulls himself through another knot of branches and comes face to face with a mother coyote. Four little pups frolic and yip behind her. In the dying light, her darting eyes are silver and serious. She lets out a low, menacing growl.

When confronting an animal one was stalking in a hunt, one learned to avoid eye contact with the animal, particularly larger mammals. It seemed to infuriate them when you looked them directly in the eye. Kaaknu can't move sideways, nor backwards, and stares her straight in the eye for a moment. In the past, he has hunted and killed coyotes with the night hunters but now he is at her mercy.

Remain calm. Don't panic. The elders' words tumble in the back of his mind. The rustling in the bramble intensifies. He averts his eyes, and the coyote and her pups silently and fortunately disappear.

He tucks himself into a cranny, sets up a small defensive perimeter, and hunkers down for the rest of the night. He listens as his rapid breathing dissipates. When his anxiety subsides, the solitude of his surroundings cuts into his heart. He fashions a rudimentary weapon out of a sharp piece of a Manzanita branch, and eats the few berries he snatched along his way through the thicket. He gathers a handful of ground insects and eats them quickly. A pair of great horned owls hoot not too far above him, comforting him—they are in trees, and the thicket didn't have trees so he must be near the edge. Under the moon, he falls soundly sleep.

When he wakes at daybreak, it is to a chorus of birds wildly chattering in the treetops. Squirrels dart about, prattling along with the birds, as if they're in a lively conversation. Crickets click; frogs croak in unison. Kaaknu feels the frenzy of life around him. He dusts off his knees and bends at his waist to crawl through the rest of the thicket and, perhaps, locate the trees from which the owls had called out.

In less than two hours, he clears the thicket and steps out onto an open grassy hillside. Daffodils spring up through the ground, bright and determined. He appreciates their beauty for a brief moment before scanning the hillside for mountain lions. They could be lurking anywhere. Their pelts blend into the autumn grass and they are known to take down elk four times their size and drag them up into trees to feast on.

Kaaknu fingers the weapon he made the night before. It is a small balm to his fears that is quickly shattered: fifty feet away from him, a golden eagle slams into the hillside, and he jumps back instinctively in fear and awe. A ground squirrel screeches in the eagle's talons. The eagle lifts its beak and looks at Kaaknu; the bird is nearly as tall as an adolescent man. With a huge and powerful slap of its ten-foot wingspan, it is off, gliding down the mountainside, the squirrel in its clutch.

Kaaknu stares after it in wonder. Never before has he been so close to an eagle—they've always soared far overhead, as if they belonged to a different world, a dimension he would never touch. Revered by all Indians, the golden eagle was a symbol of magnificence and strength. To capture or kill one was sacrilegious.

An enormous, beautiful tail feather glimmered on the grass where the eagle had just landed. Kaaknu feels with sudden assurance and clarity that it was left for him, and that he will carry it with him up the mountain and beyond. He turns, the feather in his hands, and sees the entire Volvon territory and the Black Hills plateau resplendent below him. This fresh perspective on his homeland is astonishing. To see it all at once is close to heartbreaking, given the larger forces he knows are at work.

He enters a pine forest drenched in mist that sweeps around the upper reaches of the mountain. The trees bend in the wind, creating a flute-like melody. He's seen this forest only from afar and now that he is actually in its embrace, he feels suddenly small, overpowered by the enormous pines that stretch above him towards the heavens. Only certain people have been allowed to enter this forest to harvest the pine nuts, which are not only crucial to the physical well-being of Kaaknu's Volvon tribe but also are a highly valued trade items at Brushy Peak and beyond. Mount Diablo's pine nuts are purported to possess magical proteins found nowhere else.

It's a steep climb, and he hears his pulse in his ears. Soon he leaves the band of fragrant pines and comes out upon an open rock outcrop and a loose shale ledge. One false step could lead to a thousand foot tumble. He's heard about the burials of those who weren't careful enough. Kaaknu skirts to the side, hoping he will find a serviceable crevice to ascend. But the day is against him; soon, night will fall and the outstanding panoramic vistas he's witnessed will vanish in the darkness.

With the last of the sun's rays in his eyes, he hears a sharp rattle and jumps back a full yard without thought. A rattlesnake coils mere feet from him, preparing to strike. Kaaknu lifts the walking stick he picked up in the pine forest and swings it toward the snake, deftly pinning the reptile's head to the ground. Kaaknu holds on tight. With his free hand, he pulls out his manzanita stick weapon and plunges it deep into the snake's neck. It thrashes and squirms before relenting, its body slowly losing all tension before it lies motionless on the ground. The rattles go on for a moment, and then there is silence.

Expertly he skins it and sets the skin aside to dry. He gathers twigs and starts a small fire with a handful of duff, twirling a friction stick into it. Rattlesnake steak would comprise his meal for the day. Twilight falls as he eats. The stars are so close he feels he can reach up to the sky and touch them. The moon rises in the east, shining its light across Yokut, Sierra Miwok, Patwin and Volvon territories. He sees south past the San Jose Mission grounds and into the mountains that loom over Monterey. To the north, his eyes sweep over the Central

Valley. The Sierra Nevada crests above the tule fog. It strikes him that it doesn't seem possible that the white man could ever penetrate that far into the people's territory. For now, it is still safe.

The familiar peaks of Mount Diablo stretch above him—awesome, majestic, commanding attention. Smoke lifts from a campfire far ahead of him. He knows that whoever is there can see his smoke too, and knows where he is, and knows that he is coming.

He sleeps fitfully. The sky is grey-black behind the moon, and the Milky Way swoops from horizon to horizon brilliantly in front of his eyes. Gazing out over the greater homeland, his mind races and churns. Thoughts of the white men approaching, aggressive and arrogant, make him want to cry. He is eleven, though, and too old to cry. The guns, the diseases, the loss of reliable habitat to cattle, sheep and horses—all of it is overwhelming.

And yet. And yet he knows, on his perch high up on Mount Diablo, that he will remain in Volvon territory. He and his father will let the Saclans and the Chupcans battle the invaders down in the valleys. He'll wait to be driven from his own homeland. Until then, he'll hold on to his Volvon upbringing with tenacity and continue to live in the Black Hills highlands with what is left of his people for as long as possible. It is clear now, as clear as the Milky Way, as clear as the moon.

Dawn breaks. Kaaknu has slept a little, at last. The sunrise is spectacular beyond belief. Still on his back, he marvels at the glory of the larger world. Snow gleams on the high Sierra peaks. The Central Valley is lush with wetlands.

He eats what's left of the rattlesnake meat and by the fortune of the gods, finds a spring gushing out of a crack in a rock. Pure fresh water rushes down his throat deliciously. Searching for a route past the rock outcrops he comes around a bend. The San Francisco Bay, Pacific

Ocean and Farralon Islands explode into view. He has to sit down it is so stunning a display.

The storytellers remembered thousands of years back when there was no vast bay but a great river running through world-class oak woodlands all the way out to the Farrallon Hills, which were now islands. Then came the earthquake that no one would ever forget, and everything changed. The ocean rose, the bay filled. Always be ready to adapt to the unexpected, the elders repeatedly cautioned.

The islands shimmered from far away and near them, he watched as three massive vessels slanted against the horizon, ships much more colossal than the coastal Indians were using, with huge sails. They seemed to trudge along uniformly, with great purpose, and Kaaknu knew in his heart that these ships belonged to the white men who haunted his people's dreams.

He turned away from the breathtaking and heart breaking view. At last he came upon a clear footpath. A narrow but well-defined trail beckoned. He continued on. He's heard that someone would greet him before he reached the top of the mountain and with that thought he breathes in deeply and steadies his mind. How one approached the world of the magnificent shamen was of utmost importance.

Massive outcrops materialize above him. He sees the ancient pathway trailing through slippery shale slopes and around huge boulders. The view is startling, dwarfing everything he's seen before this day. He looks left and right, forward and backward; still, there is no one to greet him. He rounds another bend in the path and the entire Central Valley and Sierra Nevada range yawns before him. He almost stumbles. He can see for hundreds of miles—north, south, and east. In front him lies a small circle of rocks with a seat carved out inside, facing due east. It is clear to Kaaknu that meditation and prayer is required at this junction, that an appropriate amount of time is meant to be spent in this circle.

He sits down. Prayer seats are not new to him; he's used them in the high hills around his village and in other villages since he was a child. But as he looks down over the land now he feels a stronger part of it, and a part of all the people. A sense of responsibility followed by a deep sadness engulfs him. The ships would move heedlessly on, he knows, even though he has lost sight of them.

At long last, he rises from the prayer seat. He wants to stay, he wants peace, but the urge to reach the top of the mountain is more urgent. He knows he is being watched, and that his progress is being monitored.

His young mind pictures the shaman and his acolytes painting their redwood-tinged skin so they could suddenly surprise him and cause his heart to leap in fear. He thinks of the young boys and grown men who had disappeared when they weren't ready for this voyage into other dimensions. Some came back catatonic and lived the rest of their lives in seclusion, with only their immediate family tending to them. But he would not be one of these. He would fulfill his birthright.

Shadows lengthen around him. The moon starts to rise behind the Sierra Nevada and it occurs to Kaaknu that it would be full tonight. He hasn't been noticing the moon's phases as closely as he should have and now he realizes that the full moon was a deliberately planned part of his journey.

He heads upward until he reaches the Devil's Elbow, an immense rock sticking up off the mountainside that he's admired all of his life. Close to the top, he stops, but only briefly, before finally reaching the actual summit. He looks around. He is still alone. A 360-degree view of his world stretches around him. The Bay Area is bathed in moonlight, and the smoke from large village fires are visible at many points around the mountain.

He senses a presence behind him. The old shaman Jalquin stands with his head raised. Jalquin, who had come to his birth, whose myths have enchanted him for years. He is dressed in tattered rags. His face is drawn; his eyes tired. He does not greet Kaaknu but points west toward the land of the Pinole tribe. A huge column of smoke swells from a cove on the edge of the bay.

"That fire is new," Jalquin says, and while Kaaknu focuses on the fire and its significance, Jalquin disappears.

Kaaknu lies down and looks up at the sky, so familiar to his eyes that it warms him like a blanket might. The sky moves slowly overhead, immutable and eternal. The mountains, the moon, the sun, the animals—all of these would persist even if Kaaknu and his people did not. The very shaman who just disappeared once told a story of the sun turning black, and then coming back, like a miracle, or a warning, or an omen. It had happened.

When he finally gets to sleep that night, he dreams he is trapped in a room with four walls that are as enormous as the rock outcrops he had passed that day. Impenetrable, impossible to climb over.

He wakes to find that a leather food pouch and a sealed goat bladder have been placed beside him in his sleep. Ravenous, exhausted, dehydrated, he is thankful for the gift of food and water and says a quick prayer before eating. The peregrine, on its morning rounds, shrieks from far below.

Morning stretches into afternoon as he waits for the shaman and his acolytes to carry out his initiation into the other worlds. The afternoon wears into evening. Kaaknu eats the last of the morsels left for him and looks out to the sea. There is no sign of the ships; there hasn't been all day. That meant only one thing: the foreigners had yet to leave. As soon as the ships were spotted coming into the bay, he knows, word spread for over a hundred miles within hours. Emergency lookouts were likely posted on every hill; runners were ready at every campsite to relay any dire news. That the three ships had not sailed back out the Golden Gate was cause for immense concern.

Far out to sea a storm brewed, dark and angry, ready to strike. The time is right—it is late autumn and storms are inevitable at this time of year. He seeks shelter in a small cave just as rain gallops to the earth. Thunder and lightning clap from the heavens, then move on. He spots smoke from a fire rising above the North Peak of the mountain, another location he has viewed all his life but never imagined he would see up close. He isn't sure if the fire is manmade or the result of the lightning. He's seen lightning strike the ground and create fires that couldn't be contained.

Time passes into the night. The fire remains stable, convincing him it must be the shaman and the acolytes. His stomach twists at the thought of them kneeling by the fire preparing food. The trail to the North Peak along the ridgeline is well-defined in the moonlight and he traverses it with ease while another round of thunder booms from the west.

A small figure is stooped by the fire when Kaaknu approaches. Jalquin. A bag of food and water is near the shaman's dirty, bare feet. He watches as Kaaknu nears the fire and lifts a gnarled hand, his fingernails long and yellow.

"Look to the north for your people," Jalquin says by way of introduction. "Look to the west for yourself. Look to the south to see the future, and look east to see your past."

With that, he stepped away from the fire and seemed to vanish. Kaaknu moved to follow him but paused. This, he knows instantly, is all that will be offered by Jalquin on this trek.

The following morning, after a night of small comforts—a fire, nourishment, water—Kaaknu heads home. He knows it is time, that he won't see Jalquin again until his next trip up Mount Diablo or at his home village in some time of need. Although it has taken him several days by circuitous route to reach the top of the mountain, it will take him only ten or twelve hours to get back to his village if he stays on the right paths. Before descending, he pauses to offer a prayer to the four directions and to repeat the shaman's last words to him.

By late afternoon, he reaches his village, after passing many villages and campsites in which the people waved but did not speak to him. They knew where he was going and that he wanted to be there without delay.

He searches the village for his mother's slender face but doesn't spot her. The village is unusually quiet and in his brief absence, it seemed to have changed, grown smaller. The difference, however subtle, bothers Kaaknu. Just south of the village a council is gathered near the sweat lodge. All are silent as he approaches. One by one they shuffle around to make space for him within their circle. His father nods at him, worry glinting in his eyes.

"I saw three ships," Kaaknu says. The men nod and stare down at their hands.

"We have heard many stories already," his father says. "We will tell them to you but first we want to know what you know."

Word of Kaaknu's return seems to have sparked life in the village. The rest of the adult villagers have gathered around the seated council, eager to listen. Clouds rolls overhead; the birds' calls die down. A chill washes over Kaaknu's skin.

He thinks for a moment of all the things he's seen in the last several days, all of the thoughts and emotions that broke inside of him. On a rock just outside the circle, a lizard captures a butterfly and hastens back to its niche to share it with its family. Kaaknu smiles, the first time he's done so since he left his village with the shaman's acolytes. The circle of life is strong, he thinks, and it will go on.

He speaks about his adventures on the mountain. Of how there was no one to greet him at the top. Of the magnificent golden eagle, the rattlesnake he ate for dinner, the coyote and her pups. Of the shaman's brief, obscure words of advice, which he knows, as he utters them again, were meant not only for him but for his whole tribe. His father nods solemnly, and turns the council's attention toward the foreign ships.

The ships had landed in Pinole Cove. The sailors set anchor and came ashore on small boats. Their ships were marveled at by the Indians—sturdy vessels with huge masts and sails that seemed to guide them directly to where they wanted to go. Immediately the sailors loaded up on water from the fresh water stream and hurried back to the ships. That night, they came ashore and started a giant fire on the beach, then waited for the tide to turn the next day and sailed back out to the ocean.

"What does this mean?" Kaaknu asks.

His father ignored his question. "The Huchiun Tribe from Pinole hid back in the hills and had a welcoming committee prepared if the timing seemed right, but the white men appeared agitated and in a hurry to return to their vessels. That is all," his father says.

But it is not all, the mood around him seems to say. The visit of the ships has heightened concerns throughout the region about what it foretold. Stories from the south were filtering north, all of them alarming.

Slowly, the elders rise from the circle and return to their wiki-ups. No one speaks. Dust rises as the group gradually disbands altogether and the daily tasks of village life resume. The women tend to their children, and weave baskets, or knead bread. The men fashion obsidian arrowheads or leave the village to hunt for game.

Kaaknu is called in to his lodge by his mother, who tells him to rest until dinner is served at dusk. He obliges, and reflects upon the days he has just experienced and the sights he has seen. His mind opens up as the earth might during a terrible rain. Lying back against his pile of rabbit skins, he feels the ground shifting beneath him, trembling under his body.

Part 3

I

The morning bursts open, white hot and dry as a bone. Kaaknu's father waits for his son near the village edge. The stern look in his eye informs Kaaknu that his father had been waiting for some time. He has overslept, again. He is now thirteen and growing rapidly. He is always ravenously hungry, and often tired.

Together he and his father make the trek to the Brushy Peak trading grounds. The sky is cloudless; the sun burning overhead. Heat steams from the ground. They are quiet as they walk and once there, his father leaves him with three bundles of goods to trade while he goes to hold council with the Chief of the Saclan tribe from Walnut Creek.

Kaaknu rests underneath a stick of a tree and smiles while he converses with his hands to trade beads, tools, spears, and herbs. He trades a pound of manzanita berries for a slab of seasoned beef from the Mission in Santa Clara. His mother has been asking for fresh shellfish lately—a request rarely made—and he scans the vendors with the hope one or two might be selling fresh oysters or clams. There is nothing, none around, he is told.

Returning to the stunted tree he's called his own for the day, he spots a young woman staring at him. He raises his chin in acknowledgement, on the verge of saying hello, when she ducks her head and retreats behind a tent filled with pottery wares created in the Missions.

A wisp of a girl, he thinks, and peers quickly behind the tent, where the girl's head is bent. The ends of her twin braids whisker at her waist and it is only at the sight of the pale pink part in her hair—so fresh and innocent, like a petal, or a seashell just washed up to shore—that he recalls the dream that disturbed his sleep the week before he was led up Mount Diablo. He has met her before, he thinks. Of course! She is Ayita, the lone daughter of the Chief of the Ssaoam tribe, who live near the Brushy Peak trading grounds and the Altamont Pass in Livermore.

"Ayita!" He calls out without thinking. She looks over at him, her ebony eyes set far apart, doe-like. "You are the daughter of Chief Ssaoa, the greatest carver of spear handles in all of the East Bay!"

She gazes at him slyly, her shyness dissolving. "And you are Kaaknu the Volvon," she says. "Son of Chief Miwok. You have battled grizzly bears on your journeys around the mountains, killed a shark in the ocean with your bare hands, and swam across the length of Lake Tahoe."

He is puzzled and nervous until she grins. Dimples dot her cheeks. She comes out from behind the tent and follows him wordlessly to his tree. She sits down in a tuft of yellowed grass and raises her right hand to shield out the sun. There is no shade to be seen.

"I know about you," she says. "Jalquin the shaman came down off the mountain for your birth."

"So I've been told," Kaaknu says. He sees this is a game and yet not a game and he wants to keep up. "Not that I can recall it," he says.

She grows serious. She is willowy and fair, with unblemished skin. "Tell me," she says just above a whisper, "what was it like way up on Mount Diablo?"

Adults mingle about them; business is to be had. But he ignores that for the moment and sits beside her and plucks a piece of the brittle grass from the ground. He tells her in detail what it was like two years before. The isolation, the fear, the uncertainty about which path to take. This he hasn't told anyone, not even his father. He tells her about the panoramic views that made him feel like a speck in the enormity of the immense world. He tells her that life has not been the same for him since he returned.

"My father says you have been given a role by the Creator," she says at long last. "That you will save your tribe from extinction."

This stuns him. He has sensed this over the years, and has gathered as much from the deference with which he's been treated by the elders, from the way he is spoken to and about, from his journey to the peak of Mount Diablo, but the boldness of her words makes him realize that he's always been carefully watched.

"My cousin is dead," Ayita says suddenly. She doesn't sigh; her voice doesn't break. It is only solemn and quiet, and this moves Kaaknu uncertainly. Speaking of the dead is forbidden, and she bends her head closer to his so others can't hear. "She was taken to the Mission in Santa Clara and she got a disease. Syphilis, I think, but my mother refuses to talk about it. They couldn't save her, even with all of their miracles and prayers and resources."

By now, in 1783, the Mission at Santa Clara had been established for over five years. Settlers were emerging in the area of San Jose, as Mexican cattle ranchers saw excellent grazing and pasture lands free and clear. Some of the tribal people from this region, Kaaknu knows, were admitting themselves into the Mission. A few saw the hard truth, that the traditional way of life was disappearing. Others saw the new, beautiful manufactured items of the Europeans and were seduced by them: they believed that a superior people had been able to produce these things and they sought to emulate this new culture and their solemn religious practices.

"I'm sorry," Kaaknu says. He looks toward the far off mountain, finding solace at its sight. Only one Volvon woman had gone to the Mission thus far. Pelna, seven years Kaaknu's senior, had fallen in love with a Santa Clara man and moved to the Mission to be with him. Kaaknu tells Ayita this.

She leans toward him. There is dust on her cheek, which suddenly endears him to her. "I've heard that if an Indian kills a stray cow for food for his family without permission from the intruders, he will be flogged. Or worse."

Kaaknu was very aware of this and it abruptly occurred to him that she had been sheltered from the most disturbing news reaching the Indian tribes daily. She looked at him questioningly before standing up and brushing off her skirt. The trading grounds had mellowed around them; the heat had relented. Soon, they would both return to their villages.

"I will see you soon I hope." she says and then she's off, her braids bouncing at her adolescent hips. To Kaaknu, this seems like a vow.

"We are going to have to send more families north," Kaaknu's father says on their trip home. "Did you notice, son, that trading from the tribes from the south has completely dried up?"

Kaaknu is considered a man now but still, he reaches for his father's forearm. His skin is wizened and thick.

"Important supplies are harder to get," his father goes on, almost flinching at his son's touch. "Thirty people to feed will be easier than a hundred, though. The Saclan chief told me today that his tribe has been resisting settler incursions with unfriendly welcoming parties. Other tribes are attacking any non-indian who nears their villages."

They are silent for some time, until they're a few hundred yards from their village.

"We will not be disturbed for now," his father says, "but protected by our tribal neighbors, the Saclans, the Chupcans, and the Ssaoams. We hold the spiritual and metaphysical tools necessary for the survival of all our people. We are the First People."

As they enter their village, Kaaknu wonders if they will be the last people. His village is deserted and ghostlike, shot through with a despairing air. He feels deflated - not because of the exhaustion of the day but of what awaits him. He thinks, where is everyone going? When will they ever come back?

II

Chief Miwok paces the ground. The day is a scorcher and sweat beads his brow. Kaaknu sighs and finally stands—his father has been pacing for what seems like hours—and grasps Miwok's hand in his own. His father gives him a bone-crunching squeeze in return and, at long last, stops. He drops to the ground and holds his head in his hands.

"This," he says, "this." Kaaknu knows his father is trying to say that this, this latest reported tragedy, is unspeakable. And it was: a runner from the Saclan tribe met one of the Chupcans in Clayton, who relayed to him the story of a well known tribe to the south. Foreigners dressed in military garb swept into their village, where close to three hundred tribal members had gathered to pray. The attack was immediate and gruesome: most of the people—men, children, women, and infants—were killed. Kaaknu thinks now of what the runner told them:

"They built a fire," the runner had said "Then they threw the tribe's sacred ceremonial dresses into the fire. Then the babies, and some were still alive. They tied weights around the necks of the dead and threw them into the nearby lake. The next day the water was red with the blood of the people."

Kaaknu knelt in the dirt beside his father. The sun seemed oppressive above them. Something pricked Kaaknu's eye and he turned to see Ayita entering the village, her body pitched forward as if in a hurry. Several feet before reaching Kaaknu, she pauses, looks at Miwok, and inches away. With Miwok's eyes still on the ground, Kaaknu waves towards the two boulders that mark the entry into the village. Ayita nods and backtracks to the boulders, where she sits with her slender legs crossed at the ankle.

"Father," Kaaknu starts, and stops. What is there to say?

"What can be done?" Miwok asks, and it occurs to Kaaknu that his father has never asked him a question that didn't have a clear and direct answer.

"I don't know," Kaaknu says. He is fourteen now, and has grown taller than his father, whose body has taken the toll of the threats from the south. The incessant worrying has carved a deep wrinkle between his eyes. And while he is still a strong man, he limps at times, his shoulders slumped, his hands visibly shaking. It is in these moments that Kaaknu turns away, as if he shouldn't see his father slip into a condition so raw, so vulnerable.

Miwok lifts his head and Kaaknu's eyes narrow in on the wrinkle. What could he say to dispel his father's worries? And when would he, as the heir to the Chief of the Volvon tribe, be responsible for the future of his tribe as his father is now? The very thought sends a shudder through Kaaknu's body.

"When the battles subside," his father starts but is interrupted by Elsu the runner, who comes towards Kaaknu and Miwok.

"Chief," Elsu says, leaning over at his waist to take deep mouthfuls of air.

"Elsu," Miwok says and stands abruptly. "What is it?"

"Ensign Gabriel Moraga is on his way," Elsu says through gasps of breath.

Miwok narrows his eyes and says with surprise, "When?"

"Soon," Elsu says. "Howi is bringing him."

"Howi?" Kaaknu says without thinking, and his father turns sharply and gives him a withering look. Kaaknu has known Howi since he was born and as the other Volvons left for the north and east, Howi was one of the few who had remained.

Elsu seems to not have noticed and continues. "They have seen Mount Diablo and the Black Hills from afar and say they've heard many stories about the Volvon territory and the First People."

"Elsu," Miwok says. "Gather the children and their mothers. Take them to the Lion's Mane village."

Elsu nods just as Muwekma returns with a satchel strapped around her chest. Miwok nods at her, and, seeming to immediately understand, she strides to Mala's wiki-up and gently urges the woman and her three children out of the village. Ayita lingers near the boulders, pulling and fussing with one of her long braids.

Kaaknu runs to her and tells her what's happened. She asks to stay with him but he tells her it may not be safe, and she starts to cry. He holds her for a moment before telling her to go, to return to her Ssaom village. "I will see you soon I hope" he says over his shoulder as he retreats back to the center of his village where his father waits. This is how they have said goodbye to one another since the first time they spoke. Before going to his father, he takes one final look at Ayita. She's already turned her back, and the last Kaaknu sees of her is the dust kicked up by her feet as she runs off towards her own village.

By mid-day, the heat is even fiercer. The village is quiet. A scattering of old people work quietly in the vicinity but otherwise, it is a shadow of their diminished village. Miwok has prepared for the meeting by donning the sacred ceremonial dress chiefs generally reserve for significant events. Kaaknu is told to do the same. From the stifling heat inside his wiki-up, he hears the clatter of horse's hooves in the grass and the insistent murmurs of a foreign tongue.

He joins his father in the center of the village, just as Howi leads, astride their horses, four men clothed in uniform trousers and shirts. The Spanish men have pushed their shirts up to their elbows, revealing sinewy muscles and skin reddened by the sun. Circles of sweat pool in their armpits. Howi's face is drawn and concerned, while the four men stride into the village with an air that suggests they own the place.

The first man to hop off his horse introduces himself, through Howi, who has learned some Spanish in Monterey, as Ensign Gabriel Moraga. He taps his hat in a gesture that implies hello, and motions to the three men behind him. Moraga offers his hand to Miwok and Miwok, in turn, shakes it. Kaaknu nods at the men, and together, the unlikely band of men walk to the mats Muwekma has set out for the meeting to take place.

A pot of acorn soup simmers on the hearth and Kaaknu signals for the men to have some. The shake their heads and lift their hands to say no. As the smallest of the men—a short, gaunt fellow with cracked, yellow teeth—takes out a small satchel of tobacco and begins rolling a cigarette in thin parchment paper, Kaaknu watches Moraga. Closely. The Ensign scans the area with what could only be described as keen interest.

Kaaknu takes in what Gabriel Moraga is taking in. The woven mats outside of the wiki-ups; the slender poles that give rise to their homes. The vistas below them, gleaming with beauty. The grand mountain itself is right there, with its thickets of forests, black now in the unrelenting sun. Joaquin smiles, a sly, telling smile, and turns to Howi.

Howi listens and then addresses Kaaknu and Miwok. "He says they are simply exploring and mapping the area for the time being." Howi's words are spoken at too loud a clip, and his lips tremble slightly.

Miwok looks at the Ensign and his men and smiles placidly. A silence descends between the men. The gaunt man extinguishes his cigarette in the dirt and leaves it there.

At long last, Moraga speaks again. He speaks in a rhythm that strikes Kaaknu as slow and condescending, as if it will take patience and a certain tone for Howi to understand his message. Howi listens with his head tilted, while Kaaknu searches Moraga's face for anything that might come close to recognition. The man's face is hollow and pockmarked with old sores and poorly-healed scars. The skin beneath his eyes is rubbery, thick, and purple. His hands are clearly strong; his nails bitten to the quick. He turns his attention, suddenly, to Kaaknu, as if he's aware he's being watched and assessed. His black eyes are penetrating and cold.

"He says," Howi starts, looking nervously between Kaaknu and Miwok's faces, "that they probably won't have much use for this area." Howi stops and bites his lip. "He also says we are welcome to remain for the time being, if we so choose." He glances quickly at Moraga, who was scrutinizing the boulders that demarcate the entry to their village, and continued "The Mission is good, this man says. They provide food and shelter for adequate survival and he says a better way of life for you under their Christian God. If we want to reconsider, we can come in at any time."

Miwok continues to smile serenely though, to Kaaknu, he seems on the verge. Of what, Kaaknu doesn't know. But, in the same fashion that he'd often seen his father act in times of stress, Miwok stands and offers his hand again. In his Volvon dialect, he asks Howi to thank Ensign Moraga and his men for their visit. And then he walks to the boulders, and with a wave of his large hand, sends them on their way.

III

Kaaknu and Miwok say nothing until the sun drops several feet, casting shadows across their bare legs. Finally, another runner, Achiote, arrives, panting in the merciless heat. He tells them that the soldier's party is now out of Volvon territory, and is headed in the direction of the Brushy Peak trading grounds.

"If they turn back," Achiote says, "we have spotters and runners ahead of them. We'll warn everyone along the way." He eats a bowl of the acorn soup quickly, and leaves without a farewell.

Still, Kaaknu and his father sit in silence, each of them coursing through their own thoughts. Kaaknu thinks of Ayita and the Brown-Eyed Susan flowers, with their bright yellow petals, that she likes to weave into her hair. He thinks of Joaquin Moraga and the other men in the party—the gaunt man with the awful teeth, the bulky man who carried his weight as if it were a threat, the man with the thin, trim mustache and the necklace that encircled his weathered old neck—and gets up. What if they take her? Steal her? Capture her, and enslave her? Rumors of the immoral acts the white men did to Indian women suddenly surged angrily through his mind and he shot up, springing to leave.

"She'll be all right," his father says, not looking up from the patch of pebbles and dirt he'd been staring at since the Moraga party left. "Her father will protect her."

Kaaknu is dubious but at least his father is talking. He sits back down.

"We are welcome to stay if we choose," his father repeats without a hint of irony. There is only sadness in his voice, and resignation.

"We're going East," a voice says, and father and son look up to find Muwekma in front of them, her arms crossed on her chest. Behind her, the rest of the villagers have trickled back. Mala and her three children, one of them on her jutting hip. Achiote's twelve-year old daughter, his three-year old son. Everyone has heard her but no one says a word.

What is meant by this intrusion, Kaaknu thinks, will reveal itself in its own time. This is their village's first direct contact with the soldiers from the south, and it astonishes him that they are living and breathing human beings, not complete monsters with bloodstains on their hands. But if they are human, he asks himself, what world do their hearts and souls reside in?

They acted like they already owned our land, Kaaknu concludes. It was this, more than perhaps seeing blood on Moraga's hands, that bothered Kaaknu the most. Anyone who'd ever questioned the Volvons' control of their territory in the Black Hills had been beaten back before they ever got anywhere near the mountain.

"We are not going East," Miwok announces loudly, interrupting Kaaknu's thoughts. "All of the surrounding tribes will band together to fend off any more unwanted intrusions." Muwekma paused at the hearth, where she was stirring a large bowl of what smelled to Kaaknu like elk stew. She peered at Miwok, and turned her head. Kaaknu knows his mother is too proud to cry.

"We are the First People, Muwekma," Miwok says. "Mount Diablo has forever been the sacred center of all of ours and our neighbors' spiritual universe. If we leave here, what will happen to our people?"

Kaaknu's mother says nothing but he knows what she's thinking. That trading with the south is now all but over. That supplies from the north—smoked salmon, dried salt, Sequoia branches for ritual fires—have to be snuck past Spanish patrols to get to the Volvon highland. That the trading ground at neardby Brushy Peak—too well-known, too accessible—has been essentially abandoned. That reports of unreasonable new settlers circulate far too often for comfortable sleep.

Howi suddenly appears back in the village, covered in dust and debris. He sits on the mat beside Miwok and removes a long splinter that had become embedded in his foot. "The soldier Moraga," he says in their native tongue, "has reportedly ordered unruly new settlers in the San Jose area to not harm the native Indians. He doesn't want an Indian uprising against the Missions. There are still too many of us in the hills."

"That's not enough," Muwekma says as she orders her son and husband and several of the villagers to eat. "There's no comfort for me in that."

"You're right," Mala whispers, taking a bowl of proffered soup. She sits down on a mat, and her dark hair falls over one eye. "It's time for more of us to go."

Miwok is silent, and not interested in his food. "I have relatives on the Merced River," Kaaknu's mother says, referring to the many intermarriages the Volvons have had with Yokut and Sierra Nevada Indians. "The winters are harsher, but that's where we'll go."

Kaaknu watches his father sit quietly as he takes in this information. Finally, the sun has set, and the air turns suddenly cold.

"I'll go there with a few others after contact has been made by the runners," Muwekma says. "Our movements will be known in advance all along the trail."

At this, Miwok slams his fist down on the table on which they're eating. Mala looks up in shock and straightens the thin piece of cloth that's wrapped around her breasts. "I have a cousin in Yosemite," she says. "If you would like that more."

"I have a relative in the Central Valley," another tribe member says.

Another lifts his hand and says, "Lake Pomo."

And yet another says, "Feather River."

"We have to make some hard choices," Achiote says, in a submissive tone, "and move on."

Kaaknu doesn't speak. Neither does his father. The meal is completed—few have truly eaten—and Kaaknu silently watches as the women take the dishes to the creek, where they will clean them and return them to their rightful places in and around their homes. The night wears on, and still, Kaaknu and Miwok sit quietly beneath the stars.

Kaaknu's resolve to remain in his homeland grows as the evening lengthens. He thinks back to when he was a child exploring the hills. The fire burning in the hearth a constant. The deer and elk herds roaming the hills. The plants that burst every year at Spring's early return, vivid in the emerald green fields. They didn't need to live in the largest village site on the widest trail, he thinks. They could move further back into the hills and canyons, where the men on horses couldn't easily find them. They could try to adapt, and change some of their ways, but stay on the mountain in the places the Volvons had discovered, nurtured, and savored for thousands of years. They could go on. They would go on.

Old camps were already set up in thorny, inaccessible places around and on Mount Diablo, Kaaknu knew. But they were now overgrown, entirely abandoned, as most of the tribe had migrated north to the other territories: Julpin, Notome, Musupum, Anizmne, and Chucmne. He could use these camps and be safe.

His father grunts beside him and attempts to stand but his back is bent forward, his arms and fingers leaning towards the ground.

Kaaknu is about to help him to bed when the thought of Ayita strikes him again: What is she experiencing in her father's circle? There is little doubt that Moraga and his soldiers arrived and departed with the same impunity and propriety they had brought into Volvon territory. The Ssoams, Kaaknu knows, will be up all night as he is now, thinking about and discussing their future, near term and long term.

Kaaknu grows light-headed—from the heat, the exhaustion, the worry—as his father stands, pats him briefly on the shoulder, and ambles towards his wiki-up, which Muwekma has lit up with a small fire outside their door. Before departing, however, he stops and picks up the butt of the cigarette Moraga's man left behind. He inspects it as he might inspect a foreign object and then stomps it into the ground, covering it completely with a mound of dirt.

Crickets stir and sing in the distance as Kaaknu thinks. He remembers what his parents have always told him, which, he is afraid, neither his mother nor his father are capable of saying now. The custom is and has forever been to reflect back upon the seven generations before you, then to look forward seven generations before deciding what the best action or non-action will be for the sake of not just you, but your entire tribe.

Constellations glittered above him; the night sky clear as day. What did the far distant past and history of his ancestors have to do with this current situation? What would looking forward offer? Nothing, it seemed to Kaaknu. The picture ahead of him was blurry, its edges mired with uncertainty. He and his family and his tribe had known a certain way of living for ten thousand years, at the precise spot where he now sat. Where they might be going seemed beyond his and his father's control or comprehension.

I will stay and meet the Europeans head on, Kaaknu thinks to himself.

But his village is too quiet, and the silence—of defeat, or of resignation—seeps into his soul. I will lurk in the hills and the upper mountain range, and remain there for as long as I can before anyone will ever find and catch up to me.

His mother would head east, and his father would follow, for what else could Miwok possibly do? He was aging rapidly, that was clear, and the next part of this battle will be completely up to Kaaknu. The rest of his people? They could go north and east, and a few—Howi among them, Kaaknu figured—would go to the Missions, with their promises of safety, lodging, and sustenance. A few would remain in the hills around Mount Diablo to fight, and Kaaknu was grateful for that. Several others, Kaaknu knewx, would merely stay and watch and wait, even as the waiting tore at their minds and hearts.

IV

Dawn breaks with a clap of thunder. Yesterday: heat; today: ferocious weather, as if the Gods above them are cautioning them for war. Kaaknu wakes with a start. He has fallen asleep on the mat near the village's central hearth. The fire is long dead but tiny embers glisten like jewels in the subdued morning light.

His father stands near the edge of their village, peering out with one hand cupped over his brow. It begins raining lightly and as Kaaknu rouses himself from the dream he was having—of dandelions and eagle feathers, with no coherent narrative—he smells the sultry, earthy scent of dirt reawakened by rain. He rakes his fingers through his long hair and rises.

"These hills are ours," his father says. He beckons towards the valley below them and the rocky outcrops above. The buttery grasslands, the wooded corridors filled with enormous, breathtaking trees. There is nothing for Kaaknu to say. He searches his mind for a word or two that might console his father.

"This rain is good for us," Kaaknu says and his father shows his agreement with a tight and decisive nod.

Chief Ssaoa calls out from the boulders below them. Miwok and Kaaknu turn at the sound of his commanding voice and invite him towards the hearth at the center of their village. Ayita lingers behind her father but looks, furtively, straight into Kaaknu's eyes. Her eyes are wildly alert and yet, somehow, tired, as if she's seen a hundred moons cross before her as she struggled, without success, to fall asleep.

Miwok leads them all to the sweat lodge, where Kaaknu and Miwok and Chief Ssaoa and Ayita, and, now, Kaaknu's mother, sleepy as she is, undress and let the warmth around them sink into their bodies. Ayita sits beside Kaaknu and tenderly takes his hand.

"Critical decisions have been made," Ayita's father says. His high forehead is magnified by the steady fire before them. He goes on to say that discussions similar to those in Kaaknu's tribe have gone on through the night. Most of Ssaoa's tribe would go north and east; the stubborn ones, he says, will stay.

"The recent tragedy down south is too close for comfort," Chief Ssaoa says wistfully. No one speaks, for the event suggested what none of them wished to admit: That they, too, might meet a similar, grisly fate.

Kaaknu squeezes Ayita's tiny hand and asks the inevitable. "And where, Chief, will your daughter go?"

Miwok and Chief Ssaoa exchange glances that speak volumes. "Kaaknu," his father says, his voice quiet and sad, but reassuring, "She will stay here. With you."

Ayita takes a deep breath beside him and grips his hand tighter.

"Most of my tribe will be gone soon," Chief Ssaoa says. "My daughter refuses to leave her homeland, but we're too visible. Too vulnerable. Too close to the Central California trade routes."

"It is time," Miwok says as Kaaknu's mother looks at him with a combination of pride and forlornness. "You and Ayita will need each other. The old ways should not get lost and become forgotten, and you two must try to hold on. We, and the other tribes, will also try to keep the Volvon people and spirit alive, and some of our ceremonies intact, but there is little else that we can do now."

As Kaaknu registers all of this, the light seems to change. It is all around him—a sudden urge to flee. His father's thigh brushes against his own as he gets up and prepares to leave. His mother will gather a few blankets for warmth on their journey; his father will take what they need to survive: the bows and arrows, enough food to make it into the Sierra Nevada, water until they reach a freshwater source.

And then they are left alone, Kaaknu and Ayita. Her father leaves with a curt goodbye; the others wave as they march away. There is little left to say. To survive, much less thrive, they must be ready and willing to accept this new order.

Part 4

I

No soldiers or settlers come into Volvon Territory for the next ten years. Reports of the miracles wrought at the numerous missions were as constant and anticipated as dawn and dusk. The hardships endured by many—beatings, kidnapping of small Indian children, the rape of their mothers by white men, disease and deaths—were also reported back to Kaaknu and Ayita who, twice a year, make the trek to Yosemite to visit their families and share the news they've received from the runners and spotters.

Miwok's health worsened in the harsher climate, and every six months, he appeared to Kaaknu as a more diminished shell of the man he once was. His mother grew thin and listless, and yet, they continued to persevere in the vast and dramatic beauty of Yosemite Valley.

And while the world around them was indeterminate, and always subject to change, the few Volvons who remained in the Black Hills adapted to a predictable curve through the seasons. Life was manageable.

Many small villages around Volvon Territory kept on functioning, though all were reduced significantly in number, as well as in spirit. They were surviving, if not exactly enjoying survival as they had in the past, while conditions to the south continued to deteriorate. Cattle now roamed freely throughout the southern hills, altering the landscape and their food supply in irredeemable ways. It was difficult—if not impossible—to imagine how and when they might be able to bring back their old practices.

Kaaknu was now twenty-four; Ayita twenty-three. They had held on since their families left, and maintained their pride of place. They had found solace in the seasons, and the annual harvesting of still plentiful acorns and berries and bulbs. Stories of tribes ravaged by disease and despair circled around them, but they and the other remaining Volvons stayed relatively untouched even as they became increasingly isolated.

Kaaknu looked over to his lovely wife. She was still beautiful, even though her eyes were darkened now with a hint of gloom: three years earlier, she and Kaaknu had a child, a baby girl they named Aiyana, which means eternal blossom. Aiyana had wide, thoughtful eyes and a smile that melted Kaaknu's heart. But it was a difficult pregnancy and a grueling delivery; after all, it was challenging to care for and nurture a pregnant woman in the shrunken circumstances in which they now lived.

Aiyana was a sickly infant, and the last remaining medicine woman was unable to procure certain medicinal herbs that had always proved useful over the centuries. Essential foods were no longer available, and the balanced diet they had enjoyed since the beginning of time in the East Bay hills was drastically disrupted. At six months, she fell asleep between Kaaknu and Ayita in their lodge, and never woke up again. After fasting and praying for six days—each day meant to represent the months she lived—they buried her near a fallen tree.

Still, some children did live, and Kaaknu took comfort in that—that his tribe could continue to reproduce. All the while the circle was closing in around them, tighter and tighter, like a noose around a man's neck. Settlers had pushed farther into San Jose, and their herds of cattle had strayed all the way into the Livermore Valley. Recently, a new Mission was built along the hills below Mission Peak in San Jose, directly on top of a nine-thousand year old Indian Village. There was little fight left in the other local tribes. They either, in an act of submission, admitted themselves into the Missions or fled north and east as Kaaknu and Ayita's people had.

Today, Mala, who had stayed in the village because of her close friendship with Ayita, comes to Kaaknu and asks to speak to him privately. "Mala," Kaaknu says, "what is it?"

Mala glances toward her three children, all of them now grown or nearly grown, as they kneel near the fire outside of their wiki-up. Her daughters are stunning; her son is blessed with the talent of dance. "I'm taking them to the Mission in San Jose," Mala says quietly.

Kaaknu frowns. He's not surprised though—she's not the first of his people to resign themselves to what they were told would be a simpler, more comfortable life.

"I'm sorry, Chief," Mala says, and he notes the desperation in her voice.

"I understand," Kaaknu says. "But you do understand that they will require you to be obedient and subservient to their God and the followers of Jesus."

"I know this," Mala says, and shakes her head as she peers around the village she's known since she was born. "I do know this."

"This changes everything," Ayita says that night as they lay in bed. What's left of their fire flickered softly in the darkness, but Ayita's face is mostly in shadow. She and Mala have been close over the years, and to lose Mala to the Missions, Kaaknu knows, is a real sign of defeat.

"The intrusion of the whites is becoming more and more frequent," Ayita adds, sitting up in bed, where the firelight picks up her more prominent features—her high cheekbones, her plump lips, her sharp nose. She was speaking specifically about the year before, when eighty settlers had set up homes in San Jose. The first active Indian resistance to Spanish military authority in the Bay Area was on the rise. Earlier in the year, Charquin the Quirostes fled the Mission at Santa Clara into the Big Sur mountains, followed by a large group of discontented Mission Indians.

"We almost always know where the intruders are and where they're going," Kaaknu says, referring to the lookouts and runners who were still in place throughout the land. "No one but Ensign Moraga has made it into our village."

"That will change," Ayita says. "It has everywhere else! What are we going to do? Wait here forever, while losing all of our people? What if it becomes just the two of us?"

Kaaknu sighed. He knew she was right. The Saclans in Lafayette continued to be unfriendly to intruders, but soon it would be time for him to go and meet the new people, at a time and place of his choosing. "We'll decide tomorrow," Kaaknu says and strokes her back, urging her to relax and fall asleep. He waits until she closes her eyes and he hears the rhythmic pace of her breathing before he leaves the wiki-up to signal Jalquin with a small fire on the overlook above the village. The great shaman will be needed.

Three days later, Kaaknu and Ayita, after many discussions, decide to visit a new encampment of settlers just outside of San Jose. They set off with a small group of warriors; Howi, who has almost completely immersed himself in the Mission life, will meet them there to interpret. It takes two long days to get there. Jalquin lurks a quarter mile behind them as they wind down the grade towards San Jose through thickets of trees and brush along the creeks in order to remain unseen.

They arrive at the ranch in the late afternoon. A high fence ⸺nds it, and snarling dogs bark and growl upon seeing them. man comes to the gate of the fence and nods.

Howi makes the introductions, his hands flying in 1

switches, now expertly, between Spanish and the language of the Volvons. Upon hearing the title Chief, the settler stands back and lifts his arms in the universal gesture of welcome.

They walk through the dusty ranch towards a camp that has clearly been constructed to be permanent. White women wearing bonnets over their fair hair linger about. A young Indian boy—who has the telling features of the Tuibun tribe—leads a heifer out to a field. There is a stillness in the air, but also a sense of excitement. Kaaknu sees young children spying on him and his group as they make their way to a large table made out of oak at the center of the compound.

There, they sit. The white man, the owner of the ranch, is named Henry. His hair is thin, the color of wheat; his eyes the pale blue of a warm winter sky. His wife Arleen joins them at the table with a plate of sliced bread and a jar of preserved raspberries. Kaaknu watches Ayita stare at the woman, taking in her alien features: the bump on her long, aristocratic nose, the freckles that dot her cheekbones, the thin, stern lips. It's the first time Kaaknu and his wife have encountered a white woman, and she is indeed a remarkable being.

They exchange pleasantries, but Henry's eyes flit often to Jalquin, who, dressed in feathers and face paint, with his medicine bag strapped across his bare, bony chest, is a commanding, intriguing, perhaps even dangerous figure. Jalquin does not sit with them, but hovers outside the gate, his eyes fixated on the group. He is there only to observe.

Ayita removes the nuts and berries she has brought the settlers as a gift, and in turn, Arleen leaves the table briefly, only to return with a small bowl full of buttons of various shapes, sizes, and colors. The women smile at one another, however tentatively. Through Howi, they learn that Henry and Arleen have four children, with another on the way. Arleen pats her stomach and gives Ayita a telling smile.

Within an hour, the conversation dies out. The bread and jam are gone, and they are given a small jar of the treat and a loaf of oatmeal bread for their trip back home. At the gate, the white people wave, and Kaaknu is grateful the meeting was short. These seekers, he thinks, have come all the way from the other side of the world to discover and overrun our beloved California. Kaaknu and his people have lived here peacefully for ten thousand years, in tune with the natural world. What was there to say?

II

Upon their return home, Kaaknu kisses Ayita softly on the forehead before he and Jalquin march straight onto the main trail to the mountaintop that Kaaknu had taken when he was eleven years old. The easier path up to the summit is the same one he came down originally, and there is some small comfort in that. But it is far less traveled and not as manicured as it once was, and this, too, is a somber reminder of how quickly and radically their lives have changed. They would take two days to make the trip that had taken Kaaknu two weeks when he was younger.

First, they stop at Louise's Shelf, which overlooks the Lower Village and the east side of the mountain. They spend the night on the shelf, praying to the mountain spirits for guidance. Jalquin and Kaaknu know that the few remaining villagers below them will leave them alone, and will keep their fires quiet to not disturb them in their quest for understanding and guidance. The night is dry and bitterly cold. They spend most of it sitting silently on the bluff, and taking turns to meditate in the sacred Walk Way, inside which they pace back and forth until almost dawn.

In the first light of morning, with only an hour of rest, Jalquin and Kaaknu descend through the Lower Village. Not a word is spoken. The few remaining people have a love and concern that is palpable in the day's early air. Down Marsh Creek they hike, heading for the Curry Creek Milling Station, where word of their quest has reached the witches, who are preparing a meal to help sustain them through the final days of their journey.

They spend the evening with the witches, sipping on their tantalizing soup, and listening to the old witches' tales of mystery and mysticism while the younger witches prepared sleeping platforms, where Jalquin and Kaaknu eventually fall asleep.

They leave the witches' home at daybreak. The ancient trail to the birthplace of the First People and the spirit gods snakes in front of them. As they climb, the sun rises in the east. They pause on their ascent to savor the awe-inspiring undulating color and light. Displays this spectacular were rare, and Kaaknu thinks it is a promising sign. While the mountain peak beckons, they stop for sustenance along the way, picking lush and perfectly ripe Manzanita berries off the trees, and catching a tasty tarantula with their hands before the spider can scamper away.

Kaaknu takes in the sights around him as they continue their climb. It is a clear, magnificent day. The world appears to him as it always has. The stunning vistas in every direction. The golden hills, and groves of oaks and bays. Squirrels scurry in the trees overhead, and, while pausing on a prominent boulder for a moment, they watch as a lizard happens upon a tiny green worm and quickly snares it with its teeth. From this outlook, it seems to Kaaknu that nothing has essentially changed.

True, new people had come and gone in the villages below, but the land, the sky, the water? They remained, and it would always be this way. These were the necessities that sustained man and all life. Without the graces of nature, there is nothing, and nature was fiercer and more powerful than any capability of man. The boulder on which they sat now was wonderfully familiar, and always would be.

People may retreat or migrate from their pockets of influence as conditions change, but life on earth would continue. The grasses may parch and regrow a different color, the trees may be cut down, as they were on the Peninsula, where ancient redwoods and oaks were being felled and burned by the new settlers, or used to construct roadways or the needs of a home: walls, roofs, tables, desks, and chairs.

A long-term drought might dry up the creek beds and lakes. It had happened. Fires could burn through all of the trees and brush on all of Mount Diablo. And yet. Mother Nature would endure. Kaaknu and the old shaman could see this clearly from their perch without talking about it.

A deep sense of relief engulfed them when they reached the mountaintop. It wasn't simply serenity, but a feeling heightened by a sense of ecstasy. Kaaknu could feel the ancient spirits in his blood, coursing through him like magic.

III

Looking west from their perch at the summit of Mount Diablo, Kaaknu pointed to Alcatraz Island in the San Francisco Bay. Tall ships skulked in the bay. "There," he says. "I want to go there."

Jalquin, a man of so few words, says, "Yes. That is the center of the new universe. It has shifted from the top of this mountain." He looks at Kaaknu. His normally rheumy, amber eyes are clear. "We will go there and pray."

They descend the mountain and make the trek through the East Bay hills to the Shellmound Village in Emeryville. The village and mound sit right on the edge of the bay. Kaaknu and Jalquin can see many other shellmounds sticking up all around the visible shores that line San Francisco Bay. There are hundreds of them, dating back to centuries unknown, each associated with its own tribe, its own villages, its own time. Our tribal Indian history, Kaaknu thinks, is irrefutable, undeniable, witness to countless generations, and it is this that breaks a smile across his face. This durability of his people.

Tule boats dot the bay, making their way around the enormous ships that both frighten and amaze Kaaknu. He's been on a tule boat several times during his life and has always been astonished by their dexterity, maneuverability, and speed. One could travel awfully fast across open water in such a boat.

He and Jalquin walk to the water, where a group of Huchiun Bay people are fishing. Through the sunlight in the fog, and with signs and a few shared words—please, help, thank you, pleasure to meet you—a young Huchiun man with deep dimples agrees to escort them to Alcatraz Island.

It will be Kaaknu's first trip to the island. Stories of the island's alchemy and exquisite powers were often discussed among his tribe when he was younger. The island was visited with some frequency by important members of all the tribes around the bay, and Miwok and Jalquin had told Kaaknu tales about their trips there.

That night the chief and shaman board a Tule boat as the young Indian man brings it close to shore. It's a dangerous passage, Kaaknu knows, requiring an expert helmsman to make the journey safely and not be swept out to sea. Also, one could never be certain where a Spaniard or settler might be and so they thought it would be best to bring the Volvon chief and shaman onto the island at night. Fires were kept low because no one wanted to attract the attention of anyone around the shore.

They set off across the bay. Fog rippled above the water, and a damp cold Kaaknu had never felt before enveloped him entirely. The young man and another skilled oars-man drop them off at the rocky east shore of Alcatraz; they would return in two days to retrieve them. Jalquin felt that the spirit of the island would take that long to present itself.

Careful of where they stepped, and carrying a small lantern with a tiny fire, they make their way to the highest point on the island. From that unique spot in the middle of the bay, they feel an isolation that they can only sense back in their village in the Black Hills. But upon looking to the right and left and all around them on the bay, they see signs of human and animal and bird life persisting. Fires burning and smoke rising from the northern shellmounds, birds screeching wildly and the timeless, endless ocean waves washing into the bay soothe them.

In the morning they wake to a splendid view of their mountain, Diablo, standing tall, resplendent, and alone in the east. To think, Kaaknu ponders, that they had been on the top of it just days before. How will the spirits further direct them?

Jalquin sits beside him and while they say nothing, it is understood that they have a shared perspective on this world. They have seen the startling immensity of it all from above. Ancient stories of past changes and environmental disasters are part of their heritage, their inner beings.

"The settled Indian way in the Bay Area is now a thing of the past," Kaaknu says.

"To look forward, we must look back," Jalquin replies. "At a certain point in every battle, one side must succumb to the other. Even though there are still battles to be fought in the Bay Area, it is time to look past that, out seven generations, to try to understand what the future might hold." With that, he waves his hand across the bay, and gestures, with his long fingers, at San Francisco. "There lies what is coming to all of us. Missions and Presidios, populated by aggressive, arrogant people."

"What are we supposed to do?" Kaaknu asks.

"We must try to understand how to survive," Jalquin says after some time. "We will try to figure out a way to keep the most important elements of our culture from disappearing altogether. Our people have been an integral part of this world since the dawn of time."

Kaaknu nods but in his heart he feels only rage. Perhaps, he thinks but does not say, the new ways and the new people won't adequately adapt to this landscape. Maybe they'll eventually crumble under their own weight and die off themselves. Clearly, the settlers and the Mission cattle have already wreaked havoc on important food sources! Could these life styles be sustainable? How many soldiers could the Spanish continue sending before all of the Mexican settlers who were showing up in droves took control of the land?

And what would life be like under them? Even in a fever of anger, as Jalquin rose and looked west towards San Francisco, Kaaknu knows. He knows he will one day be one of them. He'll be living under them as his homeland and culture are robbed from him. His village would have to be abandoned. When it was time, he and Ayita and whatever children they're blessed with will all have to go to a Mission.

But not yet.

IV

They leave Alcatraz to return to their Volvon territory two days later. No one speaks to them on their way home. Everyone knows where the two have traveled, and what has been tacitly decided. And that what they ultimately decided would affect everyone.

On their way east, they encounter a member of the Saclan tribe, who tells them that he and his men—warriors and fighters—were not planning to tone down their resistance to the settler incursions, particularly the invasions into upper-Diablo territory. They thank the kinsman, and hike on to what is still their home, for now.

Ayita embraces Kaaknu tightly when they arrive. She tells him that word of their travels to Alcatraz Island along with their visit to the settlers in San Jose, had spread rapidly throughout the Bay Area. And then, leading him to the quiet of their wiki-up, she tells him, with both remorse and excitement, that she is again pregnant. Kaaknu grabs her and clutches her face against his chest. Her hair is loose tonight, and he strokes his fingers through her long, silky tresses. Soon, he will have to tell her and the other people that the Mission life is in the future for the Volvons and all of the Indians around the Bay. Tomorrow he would do so. Tonight, he only wanted to hold his wife in his arms, and cradle her until she fell asleep.

The next morning, Kaaknu called a meeting for the adults in the village. They all sat around the hearth, which glowed with a warming fire. The day started so early that what was left of the stars still glittered above them.

"We are somewhat protected in these hills," Kaaknu begins. His people nod but glance around. They are suspicious now, always, of what might await them. Kaaknu clears his throat and tries to begin again. "This is what I've learned with Jalquin the shaman," he says, and pauses. There is fear in Ayita's eyes. He offers her a look that attempts to say, I'm sorry, but fails. "The Mission life is in the near future, for all of us."

The group is silent but several of the men and women look down at their feet, suggesting they've known this all along. Julpina, now the eldest in their community, turns to the side to hide her tears. Ayita goes to comfort her but Julpina brushes her off and speaks directly to Kaaknu, looking sharply into his eyes. "The new world does not look friendly. Not appealing," she says, emphasizing the word in an attempt at irony. "It's a world that is indifferent to our ancient ways. A world that is dangerous."

Kaaknu silently agrees with her as best as he can. The other villagers display signs of hopelessness and despair.

"Perhaps it will be temporary," he tells his people. "We don't know," he adds, lifting his hands to suggest that anything might happen. "When we go to the Missions, I will dream of the day our people can return here, to our beautiful land. For now, you should go." He turns to his wife. "Ayita and I will stay in the village and keep offering our prayers to the great creator." Ayita offers him an encouraging smile and he continues. "We will hold out until the last possible moment."

Julpina is about to say something when the runner Achiote from the Saclan tribe arrives at the boulders at the foot of their village. "Chief Kaaknu!" he yells. "A group of Spanish soldiers is on its way!"

Kaaknu rises immediately. The looks on his people's faces are desperate and afraid, and it shatters him inside. He confers with the runner on the outskirt of the village, where the Saclan tells him that the group of men—five of them—are on their way up the canyon on horseback. "There are so few outposts," the runner says, shaking his head with anguish. "They slipped past us."

"It is good of you to come here," he tells the young man, and then returns to his villagers, where he orders his people to go hide in the surrounding hills. The lookout posts could be quickly abandoned if the intruding party tried to head toward them. Ayita left with the others, tears glistening in her eyes.

Kaaknu, alone, waits for their arrival. He dresses in his full chief's regalia and feather headdress. Jalquin is watching from the hills, he knows, and that offers him some strength.

The group is dusty when they gallop in. Led by a tall soldier with burnt henna skin, Kaaknu welcomes them into his village. "I'm Sergeant DeLaveaga," the leader says and shakes Kaaknu's hand. A silver cross dangles from his neck. Howi is suddenly by his side, like an apparition, and Kaaknu shoots him a glance. Howi nods, as if to say he had heard a rumor they were coming, and knew an interpreter would be needed. A tired, old horse brays in the trees, kicking at the dirt and loose pebbles.

The Sergeant begins speaking in rapid Spanish and Howi listens intently until he is done. To Kaaknu, Howi says, "He's heard of the Volvon tribe in the hills that control Mount Diablo. Some have called this village the Garden of Eden." The Sergeant interjects, and Howi, nodding, interprets. "He says this place looks and feels very old to him and his soldiers. Very well lived in."

DeLaveaga glances around at what was left of the Volvon village. The few wiki-ups that were still in splendid shape. The countless mortars in bedrock; the fire at the center of the village spilling sweet-smelling smoke into the air. The woven mats. The intricate baskets holding blankets, animal skins, acorns and walnuts. Kaaknu feels demoralized by this man's presence in his village, hungrily eyeing the home of the First People, the place where his wife would, in the coming months, give birth to his child, a child he hoped would live and prosper in the Black Hills as he and his ancestors had for centuries.

Knowing that there were over a hundred Indians in the immediate vicinity ready to attack and brutally murder these five intruders if needed still offered him a measure of comfort and security. DeLaveaga led his men towards the hearth, where they all sat upon woven mats. Kaaknu offered them food and water, which they ravenously devoured. Howi interprets throughout the visit, and provides Kaaknu with further details. The soldiers had unfriendly encounters with the Tatcans in San Ramon and the Saclans in Walnut Creek, and realize that although it seems that Kaaknu is alone, many other Indians are around, and his group is greatly outnumbered. "They don't want to trifle with you," Howi says in a low voice. "They know you are the great Chief of the First People."

And they are respectful to Kaaknu, despite not sharing the same language. They look at him with a mix of deference and fear and wonder. Kaaknu reads their thoughts, one by one. He knows they could easily see that this was the premier village of the territory. It's very clear to all. No white man had yet been to the summit of their beloved mountain, but as the Sergeant lifted his head to admire the mountain peaks, exposing the wrinkled skin on the underside of his neck, Kaaknu knows that many yearn to. At dusk, the soldiers leave pleasantly and at will. Kaaknu breathes a long, deep sigh, and the earth seems to sigh as well.

Slowly, his people return with questions and concerns. The younger men are enraged and eager to continue protecting the only land they've ever known. Others gather their important belongings, and leave that night for safer territory. All feel robbed and raped, their privacy and tranquil lives invaded and destroyed. Ayita and Kaaknu, who have no appetite, retreat to their lodge. They fall asleep to the infuriated murmurs of the young warriors, the footsteps of those heading farther East and North, and the muted cries of the very elderly, who didn't know what to do.

V

The following year arrived with a snowstorm that swathed Mount Diablo in a breathtaking blanket of white. In the Black Hills, Ayita and Kaaknu and their new son, Kele, a sparrow of a child, continued living as they always had, though their village was a shadow of what it once was—so few remain.

On the first morning of 1796, Kaaknu layers blankets around his shoulders and ties sycamore bark around his feet and, after kissing his wife and son goodbye, sets out alone to pray on the top of the mountain. Despite the bark, his feet sink into the soft snow. The world around him is silent in this quiet storm.

Villages and camps along the way have been abandoned. Trees shake as the snow melts from their branches. There is no wind this day, only a wonderful sense of quiet in the air. His feet crunching on the snow is the only sound he hears as he ascends the mountain, save for the soft whistle of the leaves in the oaks. The animals are hiding, gathering warmth where they can. Kaaknu pauses only at moments when thirst grips his throat, and he cups the velvety snow in his mouth. Two hundred years from now, this kind of natural beauty will go on largely undisturbed, he knows.

Two days later at the summit, the air is thin, the temperature arctic. It provides Kaaknu clarity to help cast his mind forward and backward in his eternal search for guidance. He sits in the prayer circle and takes in the glorious panoramas around him. To the north is Martinez and Benicia, the Carquinez Straights and Napa and Sonoma Counties below the snow-capped Mt. Saint Helena. To the west lies San Francisco, Alcatraz Island, and far out into the Pacific Ocean the Farralon Islands. To the east, the great expanse of the Central Valley, the delta, and the Sierra Nevada range. And to the south, Mission San Jose, Henry, Arleen, and their jars of preserved berries and snarling dogs. Below him sit the Black Hills, the source of his life.

He senses someone behind him. Jalquin presses a cold hand on his shoulder, and Kaaknu rises to greet the old shaman. Jalquin has the fur of a black bear wrapped around his scraggy shoulders, a gift Kaaknu had brought to him from his father after a trip to Yosemite. The old man's eyes are tired and pained.

"Your father passed away three nights ago," he says slowly. "Before the new year."

Kaaknu cocks his head. "I can feel it. And my mother?" he asks.

"She too will pass soon," Jalquin says. "Soul mates always die within days of one another."

Kaaknu looks down at his hands, which have shrunken in the cold. His father. His mother. Will Kele his little son pass soon as well? Or will he make it through this winter, and many more?

"It is time, Chief Kaaknu," Jalquin says sadly. "There is no time left for celebrations. Our people are disrupted, dispersed. We must go now, to the New World."

"We could still hide in the Vasco Caves," Kaaknu says weakly.

"Demoralization and depression continue to set in upon our people", the shaman continues. "No spiritual seekers from other tribes still come to the mountain. Ayita and Kele will go with you wherever you choose."

Jalquin gazes at Kaaknu and then slowly extends his arms and spins around in a full circle, indicating the immeasurable views in every direction. Where once there was smoke from village fires as far as their eyes could see, now the fires were sparse, and few and far between. Except for the smoke from the Missions in San Jose, Santa Clara, and San Francisco. That's where there was light; that's where there was now human life.

The shaman points at the enormous billows of smoke coming from San Francisco, and, saying nothing, heads off in that direction, his bare feet sliding through the snow. A ray of sunlight suddenly appears, breaking the calm of the landscape, and Kaaknu gets up. He knows what he has to do, and that is to make personal contact with the missionaries and soldiers. It was either that, or continue to wait in fear for them to come after him. He set off back to his village, the present vanishing in his eyes, the future beckoning, however bleakly.

"We will go to visit the Missions when the weather clears," he tells Ayita upon his arrival home. She has Kele at her breast, whom she watches very closely, and without looking up, nods.

One week later, they began their journey to San Francisco. Accompanied by several warriors, hunters, and traders, and equipped with an ample supply of provisions—how long they would be gone, and whether or not they would return was unclear—they hiked towards the swells of smoke they could see in the distance.

"Will we ever come back?" Ayita asks softly. Kele is strapped to her stomach, looking out across the expanse of land.

Kaaknu had heard of Indians being held at the Missions against their will but he shook his head confidently. They still had friends and supporters he knew. For her to enter this situation too worried would taint their visit.

All of the villages and campsites along the way to San Jose are abandoned. Bedrock mortars are filled with dead leaves; the carefully woven covers of some of the wiki-ups flutter forlornly in the breeze. Hearths are cold, or filled with water from the recent rains. Dance lodges sit lonely and in disrepair.

They arrive at Mission San Jose the next morning. Bells chime in the distance; cattle wander freely. Several of their Volvon people who have submitted themselves to the Mission life run up to them. A few have huge smiles on their faces; others cling to them desperately. One has a black eye and when Ayita asks about it in a low voice, the man bows his head and returns to the fields.

A horse-drawn wagon appears, and Kaaknu, Ayita, and their group look at it in awe. From the carriage steps out a man wearing long, tailored clothes and a hat on his head. When he takes it off, Kaaknu sees wheat-colored hair. It is Henry the settler, who, it appears, has joined the Mission as well. He walks towards Kaaknu and bows a tad at his waist in greeting. Several padres and other settlers gather around, and nod at Kaaknu with deep respect. Henry says, "They all know who you are, Chief Kaaknu. And what you represent. You are welcome here."

Replenished with food and water, they leave within two hours for their next destination: the Mission Dolores in San Francisco. Kaaknu and his band of travelers are silent as they walk. They spot several cows but see no sign of deer or elk. Some of the old village sites and campgrounds have been burnt to the ground, and the smell of decay and burnt wood saturates the air.

During their travels, they stop and camp at night off the main pathways, hoping and praying they'll be left alone. It's clear that word, by this time, has spread from San Jose to San Francisco that the Volvon chief's group are on their way. They aren't going to surprise anyone. Still, they humbly keep a low profile. Once a day, a group of wagons and soldiers on horses clatter by them, barely noticing nor acknowledging their small party.

That evening, Kaaknu and Ayita lay under the dazzling stars. The constellations are where they've always been but to Kaaknu, they look unfamiliar and threatening.

"Goodnight, Kele," he whispers to his sleeping son, and rolls over, hoping they will at least be blessed with some rest in spite of all the disturbing thoughts swirling in their minds.

VI

The fog lays heavy on the land as they make their final approach to Mission Dolores. They climb hills thick with Kelly green grass under the darkened sky, and pass Missionized Indians gathering wood and carrying buckets of water in the same direction they are headed. Through the fog, they catch glimpses of the famous Mission. Constructed out of logs, thatch, and adobe, the long building sits at the edge of a large creek. The water in the creek looks black in the dim, hazy light.

Gunshots suddenly ring out in the near distance, stopping them in their tracks. Pulses quicken. The baby begins to bawl. The small group doesn't move, uncertain of what awaits them. At long last, several Ohlone Indians scurry by, dragging a bloodied, dead horse into one of the outlying buildings.

They walk further. No one smiles at them or greets them, but many nod directly at Kaaknu, as if they've been waiting for him. Soon, a padre and a soldier come out to meet them and lead them through an orchard of fruit trees lined up in perfect rows. This sight is new to Kaaknu and his people. Random acts of nature have always guided their management of food resources but to see this, this deliberate planting and nurturing, impresses and confuses him. It seems so premeditated, too orderly, out of tune with the way trees grow untended in nature.

Without speaking, the padre leads them further into the compound. The Mission is abuzz with work and energy, yet a listlessness is sensed in the slumped shoulders of the older Indians. Inside the chapel a large mural depicts Indians performing hard labor in a farming field. San Francisco Bay is in the background, gray and austere. Jolon, an old Volvon tribe-mate, suddenly appears and nods indifferently but respectfully at Kaaknu and Ayita. He has changed, Kaaknu sees. He's dressed in the clothes of the white people, and his hair is cut short. A crucifix is tied with a piece of black string around his neck.

"I am here to interpret for you," he says in the Volvon dialect. Gesturing with open arms at the chapel and the business being conducted outside, he proudly declares "This is Mission Dolores. Soon you will meet the founder, Junipero Serra. And this," he says, motioning to the soldier who accompanied them into the Mission earlier, "is Captain Jose Arguello."

Arguello stands silently off to the side, dressed entirely in military garb, and quickly straightens his shoulders as a thin frail looking man dressed in a brown robe strolls into the chapel.

"Father Junipero Serra," Jolon says, and bows at his waist. The Father's hair is thinning at the side, and his eyes, beady and sharp, scan Kaaknu and his people with interest. He strides toward them without a hint of a smile, his thin, dry lips in a tight line.

"When are you going to come and bring in the rest of your people?" Serra inquires through Jolon.

Kaaknu doesn't reply. He looks at Jolon with what he hopes is a mask of confusion and misunderstanding. This level of incivility is uncalled for.

"Unrepentant savages," Serra mutters to himself and coughing, dismisses them with a wave of his hand.

"Come with me," Jolon says and together, with Arguello, they tour the Mission grounds. The people from Kaaknu's village who had come here years before barely raise their heads so immersed are they in the tasks at hand. They enter a room in which enormous ovens are being used to create iron metal which, Jolon says, the blacksmiths will use to make their own farming tools. Horses hitched to plows whinny and shake their tails. Whole fields in the distance are being churned upside down. Large parcels are crowded with food crops, many of which he's never seen before. He smells fennel, chamomile, irises.

Nearing what Jolon calls the "dining hall," Oya, who Kaaknu has known since they were children, leaps up from shucking corn and grabs onto Kaaknu. "Chief," he cries. "Take me home!" Arguello swiftly and seemingly without thinking rams the butt of his rifle on the back of Oya's head and yells at him, pointing viciously at the corn. Oya turns without hesitation and returns to his work. Ayita's eyes open wide in shock.

The aroma of fresh cooking fills the dining hall, where many people are gathered, eating quickly. Kaaknu and his family are given a meal of roasted lamb, garbanzo beans, and bread. But they are told to eat quickly, and are then shown to the quarters they've been assigned during their stay in the Mission.

Their living quarters are a donkey stall that reeks of urine and waste. The donkey, Kaaknu imagines, has only recently been taken elsewhere, and he feels hatred slicing through him, like an obsidian spearhead to his gut. He peers around—at the hay on the ground, at the mud on the walls, at the canteen near the corner, holding water that's buzzing with flies—when Jalquin turns the corner, arriving, as he always does, unannounced, flitting through places as a supernatural being might.

"Jalquin," Kaaknu says breathlessly. He had last seen Jalquin marching down the mountain towards San Francisco but he'd never really imagined he'd see the old shaman in such a place as this. To Kaaknu, it always seemed that Jalquin would remain at the Shaman's Redoubt on the summit of Mount Diablo until his death, and his spirit would live long after that.

Jalquin says nothing but goes to Kele and whispers a quiet chant that makes the baby smile curiously at him. Ayita hands the child to him and Jalquin, whose eyes were once so fierce and defiant, now looks distraught even as he cradles Kele and speaks softly and kindly to him. Gone, it seems, is his profound determination to live out his final days where he belongs: in Volvon Territory on Mount Diablo.

VII

After a sleepless night, Kaaknu, Ayita, Kele, and the rest of their small group get up to leave. Kaaknu doesn't see Jolon on their way out, but gives a nod of appreciation to Arguello, who stands stoically at the entrance to the Mission compound with a rifle strapped across his chest.

As Kaaknu leads the way in the violet light, his son fastened to his shoulders, he thinks that he will not become like Jalquin. He will remain a proud Volvon and refuse to succumb entirely to the new ways. They would have to return to the Mission one day, he knew, but hopefully on better terms than had greeted them this time.

It takes them five days to return to the Black Hills. Kaaknu's people—what's left of them in their still glorious natural environment—appear tired, as if they haven't slept since Kaaknu's departure. He notes that new hiding places have been carved into the hills surrounding their village. Without his presence there, he knows, they were agonizing about the possibility of intruders, if not violent death. He slowly leads the few left in his village to the central hearth, where Ayita rekindles the fire.

"Time is not on our side," He says. His people know; they've been anticipating this for so many years. He goes on to tell them about what his family and warriors had experienced along the way. About the abandoned villages. The donkey stall in which they slept. The groomed fruit trees, and the Mission Indians working until their hands bled. Of Father Junipero Serra.

"Tomorrow," Kaaknu says, "we will move to the Lion's Mane Village. We'll start to cover up all of the conspicuous trails leading into and out of it."

"I'm going to the Mission in San Jose," one of the female tribal members says. "I can't stay here, Chief. I'm expecting a child and I need to do what I can for the baby to survive."

"I understand and appreciate that," Kaaknu says, and, after a brief meal with all of the tribe, he and Ayita draw away from the group and settle in in their lodge with Kele. Kaaknu glances around at the home he has known for so many years, and an unspeakable sadness consumes him. He has three options, and three options only: to hide in the hills indefinitely until they are forced out at gunpoint, to flee North or East, or return to the Missions and be amongst most of his people.

Ayita washes her face and lies beside him on the stack of rabbit furs. She lifts the cloth she wore as a dress to the Missions and smiles coyly at Kaaknu. Kaaknu sees, and then feels, the curve of her stomach. He presses his hands against its hard surface, and feels the new life, fluttering ever so gently inside of her.

Part 5

I

Kaaknu wakes to another spectacular colorful sky shining into his wiki-up. He is alone. Outside he hears Kele speaking quickly but scornfully to his mother. He is almost a teenager, soon to be a man, and his moods in the latest seasons have ranged from ecstatic to melancholy, seemingly with no reason. He hears the squawk of his daughter, Enola, her gleeful laughter. Surely, she is with one of the fawns that come often to the edge of the Lion's Mane Village to forage whatever food they have left over. He remains still for a moment, enjoying the sounds, the smell of acorn bread baking, and the admonishments of his wife to his son. As far as Kaaknu can tell, Kele wants to go with one of Jalquin's former acolytes to see what's new in Walnut Creek.

He stretches when he finally stands, and lifts the flap of his wiki-up to take in the day. Ayita throws him a sassy, exasperated smile over her shoulder. His daughter grins. His son sighs moodily and heads toward the trees, where he will spend the next several hours practicing carving manzanita branches into hand tools.

It has been twelve years since Kaaknu and Ayita went to the Mission Dolores. Twelve years of anticipating the worst, and surviving on what little food they could scavenge, and yet twelve years of mostly uninterrupted bliss.

Several years earlier, news of the Saclan tribe's fate made its way to Kaaknu's village. Due to oppressive conditions and rampant disease, two hundred and eighty Saclans had fled Mission Dolores and headed to what they hoped would be safe harbor in Napa County. Pursued by Presidio soldiers and Indian guides, a tremendous battle ensued in the Napa Valley. There, several of the Mission posse were killed and the rest driven back to San Francisco; still, the Walnut Creek Saclans in Napa didn't dare return to their villages in the Diablo Valley, just below the sacred mountain.

Without the Saclans' protection, soldiers and settlers pushed further and further north towards Volvon territory. At night, during the prior twelve years, Ayita or Kaaknu or Kele or Elona or all four of them would wake with a shudder at the sound of horse hooves in the distance, and the yells of foreign men, while they remained hidden in the Black Hills. But on any given morning, a lone Indian from one of the many shrunken Bay Area tribes would arrive, seeking shelter and sustenance, and would remind Kaaknu that he was still revered throughout the land.

Shortly after the war in Napa, a gang of soldiers and Indian guides came into the Diablo Valley, searching for escaped Mission Indians. They were confronted by a group of warriors at the Willow Grove in Concord, on the north side of Mount Diablo. Another deadly battle ensued led by the Chupcans from Clayton, until Kaaknu appeared in full ceremonial regalia. The very sight of him sent tremors of fear through the soldiers and the native combatants. Prudent, uncertain, and wary of the importance and powers of Kaaknu the Volvon, they all fled in opposite directions. Everyone had heard the legends and mysteries associated with the mountain people, the Volvons.

Despite the terrors and the unease, Kaaknu and his family were content. In the past twelve years, they'd traveled twice to visit the Missions in San Jose and San Francisco, but always on their own accord, and always allowing themselves enough time to pay homage to the giant redwood in Palo Alto. There, they would pause to pray and to embrace the natural world, in all of its glory and complications and timelessness. The children liked to rub their backs against the trunk of the ancient tree, and watch as sunlight dappled their faces and arms and legs through the high branches. During those moments, Kaaknu and Ayita would share an embrace also, tucked beneath the shaded, scented canopy of the majestic tree.

Kaaknu, sitting at home with Ayita as he's given a mug of warm tea made of elderberry bark, chamomile blossoms and peppermint leaves, looks around, saying nothing. This is how he will remember his ancestors. This is how he will remember his tribal territory, even though they will soon leave this beloved land for the New World. Tomorrow he will go to Yosemite with his son to leave flowers on his parents' graves. And after that, he and Kele will go to Mission Dolores to pick up Jalquin's remains and bury him, after a week of prayer, at the summit of Mount Diablo.

And in a month or two, perhaps more, he and his family and the few Volvons who remain in the village will bury their sacred belongings under the dirt at the Lion's Mane Village and leave it forever. They will go to Mission Dolores and learn to live as the new people have. They will work, they will eat, they will sleep, they will make love, they will procreate. And while mired in the ways of the New World, Kaaknu, the last Chief of the First People, will, whenever possible, remind his people of the ways of the past.

But for now, he is content. The Manzanita berries hang lush and ripe from the trees. Acorns droop from the oaks. The sky is flawless, a vivid cerulean blue. And his children, his daughter now at her brother's side, tickling his ribs, laugh together, a sound, to Kaaknu, like no other. This is how he will remember everything. He will remember *all ten thousand years of this life.*

Epilogue

The years passed slowly. The landscape changed, politics in the Missions altered dramatically, the people of California and across the world were forced to accept the constantly shifting ways of modern life. The vibrant native Indian life diminished. The Spanish and Jesuits withdrew from several of their commitments on the West Coast and the decision was made to close Mission Dolores in San Francisco and move the remaining Indians to Mission San Jose. Kaaknu and his family were among them.

On the journey from San Francisco to San Jose, Kaaknu made his way towards the magnificent redwood tree in Palo Alto. The tree was gone, and in its place sat a huge stump. The sight of it dismayed Kaaknu, but upon further investigation he discovered forty new shoots sprouting around the felled trunk. For a moment, he was elated, and it was there, peering at the shoots, that he decided he would use the undeniable resilience of the redwoods to illustrate to his remaining people that life would go on, and the Volvon ethos would live on, in spite of the countless obstacles they would inevitably encounter.

Four years later, Kaaknu the Volvon, the great falcon chief, died at Mission San Jose in a plain, windowless room, in his sleep. He was fifty-six, an old man.

Prior to his death in 1826, Kaaknu would return to Mount Diablo annually, where he prayed and thanked the Creator for all the blessed life around and within him. When his second son had been born at the Mission in 1805 he was adopted as the god son of the soldier Arguello, which established an important dynamic that prevailed in the relationship between Kaaknu and his tribe and the Spanish and the Missionaries and the settlers. He had commanded the attention and respect of his captors.

Kaaknu the Volvon Chief and the highest levels of the modern Europeans were essentially acknowledged to be equals as human beings. The process that allowed this to occur and the emotional depth of this integration of culture was a seed that wouldn't be brought to life for a century and a half. His second son had died three months after he was born, leaving in Ayita a well of sadness that would persist until her passing, twenty years later, six months after Kaaknu's demise.

Today, Kaaknu's Volvon homeland remains virtually intact and undisturbed. The stunning vistas and the magical perspectives that made Mount Diablo sacred are still there. The village and camp sites, the copses of manzanita, oaks, and pines, the mountain lions and eagles, and the great, vast beauty all endure. When Kaaknu left it for the last time, he hoped he wouldn't be gone for long. The peregrine falcons still soared over the Volvon Territory, as they always had.

Map
Of The Volvon Territory

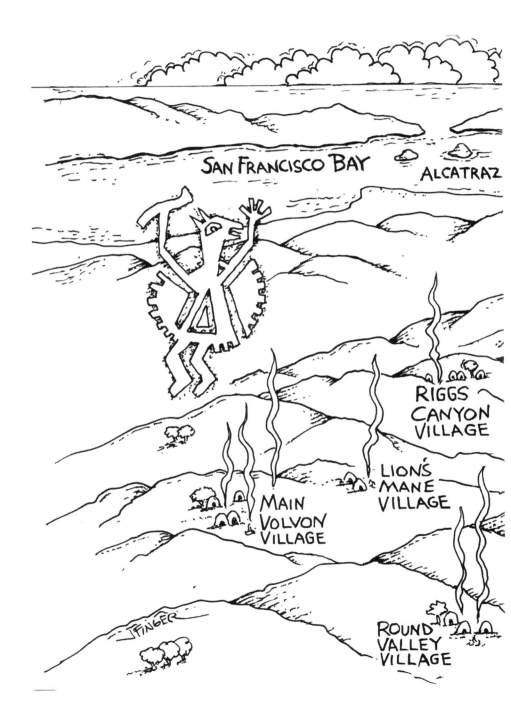

Notes:

KAAKNU THE VOLVON

Notes:

KAAKNU THE VOLVON

Notes:

KAAKNU THE VOLVON

Notes:

Notes: